War of Dragons

Wingman 22

Books by Mack Maloney

Mack Maloney's Haunted Universe
Iron Star
Thunder Alley

Starhawk *series*
Starhawk
Planet America
The Fourth Empire
Battle at Zero Point
Storm Over Saturn

Chopper Ops *series*
Chopper Ops
Zero Red
Shuttle Down

Strikemasters *series*
Strikemasters
Rogue War
Fulcrum

Storm Birds *series*
Desert Lightning
Thunder from Heaven
The Gathering Storm

War of Dragons

Wingman 22

Mack Maloney

*For my good friend Anita
Best of Luck always*

Mack Maloney

SPEAKING VOLUMES, LLC
NAPLES, FLORIDA
2023

War of Dragons

Copyright © 2023 by Mack Maloney

All rights reserved. No part of this book may be reproduced or transmitted in any form or by any means without written permission.

ISBN 978-1-64540-844-4

In Memory of Mr. Bruynell,
a really good guy

PART ONE

Chapter One

Gibraltar

It was exactly midnight when the doors to the small police station burst open and the mob of villagers rushed in.

Carrying torches, pitchforks and shotguns, they started banging on the front desk, loudly demanding attention.

Two policemen were on duty in the back; one had been asleep, the other reading an old porn magazine. Both had been drinking. Up until now it had been a quiet night. Only about five hundred people lived in Gibraltar these days. It had become a very sleepy place since the Big War and nothing of any consequence had happened here in years. Most people survived on fish they caught themselves and things like electricity and clean water were spotty at best. The police force wasn't even a police force; it was made up of four local gunmen earning some money on the side.

The villagers were in a panic. With three or four talking at once, they told the policemen a fantastic story: a strange creature was flying around the top of the Big Rock. They'd all seen it. It was making a horrible buzzing sound and was leaving great balls of fire in its wake.

The policemen barely moved. Drunkenness and drug use was rampant in the small settlement and that seemed to be the case here. They ordered the crowd to disburse, go home and sleep it off. But the villagers were adamant. They physically dragged the two skeptical policemen over the front desk, through the front door and out onto the street. Then they made them both look up at Gibraltar's peak, 1,400 feet overhead.

The policemen were stunned. Something was indeed circling the top of the Big Rock. The villagers were jabbering that it was a large bird. Stories of a giant winged creature haunting Gibraltar's summit had sprung up over the years—and now, here it was.

But the policemen knew better. This was no bird. It was an airplane. Very small, more bug-like than feathered, but unmistakably powered by an engine, a very loud and smoky one.

One policeman ran back into the station and returned with a primitive NightVision device called a Starscope. It could both see in the dark and zoom in on objects far away. He aimed it at the peak—and now saw the bizarre aircraft up close. It was going around the top of the mountain at high speed, its wind-tips almost scrapping against the Big Rock itself. But then every few seconds the diminutive craft would come to a complete stop and point its nose almost straight up. Its propeller acting now more like a helicopter's rotor, it would hover for a moment or two, almost as if it was looking for something. Then it would slam back down to level flight, let out a horrendous screech and dash away in a flash of fire and smoke.

It was the strangest thing the policeman had ever seen.

At least so far.

Suddenly the little plane disappeared. One moment it was there; the next, it was gone. But its unnerving buzzing sound was replaced by something more unsettling: a deep, growling noise coming from the famous strait nearby. The policeman turned his Starscope in that direction and immediately caught something in his lens.

Six boats were coming in from the Atlantic side, barely visible in the weak light of the quarter moon. He zoomed in further to see they were tugboats. All in a perfect line, they were heading towards a small dock in the harbor right below them. The policeman zoomed-in all the way and saw heavily armed soldiers in night camouflage gear were gathered on their decks, ready to disembark.

"Someone is invading us?" he asked out loud. "In…tugboats?"

An instant later, the night was filled with yet another terrible screech; it was so loud everyone in the street immediately blocked their ears. They turned as one to see the strange little flying machine they'd spotted circling the Rock earlier was now hanging just a few feet off the ground right behind them.

They were petrified. This thing looked like something from a demented circus. It was absurdly small except for its tires, which were absurdly big. The pilot was dressed like a character from a comic book; everything he wore was exaggerated, from his oversized crash helmet to his giant bug-like flight goggles to his bulked-up super-hero flight suit. Even the giant banana-clipped hybrid M-16 jammed inside the cockpit with him seemed more like a movie prop than a real weapon. The whole thing looked frightening but illogical at the same time.

The villagers fled. Dropping their torches and pitchforks, they quickly disappeared into the night. The policemen remained frozen to the spot, though, unable to move. The pilot was looking at them very intently, as if sending them a message, non-verbally, maybe even psychically.

Either way, his meaning was clear: Time to go.

Throwing their weapons aside, the policemen finally ran off too, praying aloud the weird little airplane would not follow them.

*****

The six tugboats reached the small dock moments later. With great precision, thirty figures climbed off the vessels, faces blackened, two squads of fifteen men each. They were bristling with weapons but under unusual orders not to be wearing aftershave or carrying food of any kind.

The Big Rock's cable-car was long gone, destroyed by parties unknown. So the soldiers streamed through the Jews' Gate and up to the Mediterranean Steps. A dozen flights of extra steep stairways lay ahead. It was almost a half mile to the top of Gibraltar, a lot of it nearly straight up.

As each soldier was equipped with NightVision goggles, they quickly became aware that many eyes were watching them from the dark foliage on either side of the steps. This was no surprise. But as instructed, the soldiers kept their own eyes forward, weapons ready, but safeties on.

Then a helicopter suddenly appeared out of the darkness above them, a large wooden box dangling beneath its fuselage. It flew over the troops and then dropped the box, intentionally allowing it to smash into the ground. It split open to reveal hundreds of bananas inside.

There was an eruption of sound and crashing as dozens of dark creatures launched themselves out of the foliage and towards the broken crate of fruit. They were Barbary macaques, the famous Gibraltar monkeys. The undisputed rulers of the Big Rock's summit, they were known to attack humans carrying food, or if they smelled offensive to them—or if they were invading their turf.

The air drop of bananas changed all that. The entire gang of them, easily three hundred or more, pounced on the sudden pile of fruit and began gorging themselves, completely forgetting the soldiers in their midst. The animals thus distracted, the soldiers started to climb.

Up they went, one long stairway after another, until they finally reached the last set of steps leading to the top of the great rock. Half the soldiers created a security perimeter here, while the others geared-up for the last leg of the ascent. The noise of this preparation was momentarily drowned out by a deafening roar. Suddenly the small clown plane came out of the night. It landed hard on the side of the hill in one, two, three bounces, stopping about fifty feet from the soldiers.

The tiny canopy opened and the pilot squeezed out. Retrieving his banana-clip M-16, he took off his extra-large helmet and pushed back his nearly shoulder length hair. It was Hawk Hunter, the Wingman. He was the commander of this odd mission.

He took a look around. The giant foreboding peak, the long sets of steps to the top, the troopers waiting nearby, the gluttonous monkeys far, far below.

"This must be the place," he said to himself.

Anticipating this strange operation, Hunter had rebuilt his famous clown plane from nearly scratch, doing so in just two days. It looked like an old Piper Cub shrunken down to one quarter size, with everything being appropriately elf-friendly, except the gigantic tires. Preposterous as an aircraft and a wonder it could even fly, it could take off and land in just a few feet and so it had been essential for what they were doing here tonight.

The 30-man assault team was part of the long-time United American special ops group known as JAWS. They were specialists in mountain warfare and Hunter had worked with them more times than he could count. Their CO, Hunter's old friend, Captain Jim Cook, was carrying a large circular antenna resembling a hula hoop. Weird as it looked, the "Boop" could locate the source of any radio transmission within a half-mile radius.

With Hunter and Cook in the lead, the summit team went up the last stairway, taking the steps two at a time. It was a very windy climb. Gales of sand were blowing in from North Africa just across the strait and the higher they went, the more barren the landscape became. Soon the foliage disappeared completely and they were surrounded by bare ground, gangs of huge boulders and plenty of sharp smaller rocks.

But it was at the very peak that they found the oddest thing of all: a small chicken coop tottering on the southern edge of the enormous limestone outcrop. The Boop radio detection gear started buzzing and its contact light clicked on the moment they spotted it.

Fighting howling gusts, goggles down to see through the clouds of sand, the assault team set up a quick perimeter around the coop. Then, with Cook at his side, Hunter gingerly opened the coop's door to find one lone chicken inside, tethered to its nest. Startled by the sudden attention, the bird began squawking mightily. Meanwhile, the Boop continued buzzing and now its contact light was burning red hot.

Hunter looked up to Cook, who just nodded.

"Something's underneath," he told Hunter.

The Wingman carefully lifted the bird's nest to find a large circular-shaped, 3.5 kiloton nuclear bomb, ticking softly.

Hunter couldn't believe it.

"Goddam," he gasped. "She was right . . ."

Chapter Two

They called it Spookytown.

It was a large compartment deep within the USS *USA*, the gigantic, renamed Russian-built aircraft carrier captured by the United Americans three years before.

Every person aboard the highly automated ship had a security clearance; it was a requirement for duty on the big carrier. Even so, of the now thousand member crew, only a couple dozen had access to Spookytown. Entry was strictly on a need-to-know basis.

Its official name was the Special Purpose Offshore Operations Command room, or the SPOOC. At five hundred square feet, a large compartment for any ship, it was in fact a floating field office for the United American Intelligence Agency, America's post-Big War CIA. Because the UAIA's highly-respected spies were known around the world as the Spooks, this place became known as Spookytown.

The center of the Spookytown universe was a huge lighted planning table with two dozen chairs around it. At the moment, each chair was taken by someone high-up in the ship's command structure—except one. In the seat at the head of the table was the recently liberated chicken, plucked from the top of Gibraltar. Now untethered and living in a portable cage, it was working on a loaf of bread, clucking softly, unaware of its place of honor.

The debriefing for the recently completed Gibraltar operation was underway. Captain Cook of the JAWS team was giving a first-hand account of what happened on the Big Rock. Starting with the amphibious landing via the carrier's protective force of armed tugboats, known to all as the Slugboats, to reaching the peak and disabling the nuclear device, the mission had been flawless.

"From what we could see," Cook explained, "the chicken was a way to keep the nuke warm and still operational even if the power went out down below. We found evidence that one of the local families was paid by persons unknown to climb the rock every four or five days and feed the chicken, no questions asked."

Cook glanced at the bird, very content in its new home. "We just thought it was best to bring it with us," he said.

The monstrously-sized USS *USA* had transited the Panama Canal two weeks before, fresh from a Pacific foray that included two small wars and more combat than anyone on-board cared to remember. Though long overdue for replenishment and a refit, it had rushed instead to its present location just off the Atlantic coast of Gibraltar as soon as the potential for a grave nuclear crisis had been uncovered.

But recovering the Chicken-Coop Bomb was just the first step in what was about to become the UA's most dangerous mission ever. And though weary and in need of a paint job, they believed they had just the right warship for what lay ahead.

In many ways the USS *USA* was actually a hybrid vessel. True, it was home to nearly one hundred warplanes and helicopters, more airpower than the vast majority of countries around the world these days. But the ship also carried two giant 18-inch gun batteries fore and aft, two dozen SAM batteries on both sides of its flight deck, plus a half dozen CIWS turrets, essentially modern Gatling guns that could spit out an astounding 50 rounds *a second*.

The ship's command team was made up of the same group of warriors who'd thrown the Russians out of America, flattened the Moscow-controlled city of Hamburg, and most recently, dropped a nuke of their own on Tokyo Harbor. Bull Dozer, Captain Crunch, The Cobra Brothers, Major René Frost, the JAWS guys, Ben Wa, "Socket' Toomey—and Hawk Hunter. They'd all been doing this a *long* time. Saving the world was second nature to them now.

But again, the challenge this time was to be the biggest yet: prevent a world catastrophe so enormously large, it would make the Big War seem like a slap-fight, and their own recent A-bomb drop a mere firecracker.

To complete this mission, though, they had to catch a ghost.

His name was Viktor Robotov.

The world's bogey man since the end of the Big War, the ex-KGB super-spy had brought untold misery to the decimated planet for no other reason than he'd enjoyed watching others suffer. It was his atomic weapons factory in Tokyo Harbor that the UA nuked with hopes of catching the uber-villain in the blast, only to see him escape at the last instant. This led to a thousand mile chase which ended when Viktor was killed trying to get away in the Zon space shuttle, something he'd done successfully at least once before.

But the Devil never goes quietly. In the months before he died, Viktor arranged to have six nuclear mines hidden in places of his choosing, foreshadowing his own demise long before it actually happened. His goal: to go out with an irreversible cataclysmic multi-megaton bang—and take the planet with him.

Chapter Three

Hawk Hunter had a serious caffeine addiction.

Upon returning to the USS *USA* after the Gibraltar operation and landing the clown plane on its vast deck, he went not to Spookytown first, but to the ship's starboard galley where he requisitioned an entire pot of coffee for himself. Only then did he proceed to the SPOOC. The coffee was gone by the end of the mission debriefing.

As the meeting broke up and the participants headed to get chow, Bull Dozer caught Hunter leaving the SPOOC, empty coffee pot in hand. One of the original United American commanders, Dozer was well-named as he was a bulldozer of a man. He'd been commander of the legendary 7th Cavalry assault group for more than a decade. But in just the past few years or so he'd led UA forces against the Russian occupiers of New York City, then had served as mayor of that same city, *then* became captain of the massive USS *USA*.

He'd done all three jobs admirably. But above all, he had no illusions about what lay ahead of them now.

"Can you live without that stuff for about twenty more minutes?" he asked the Wingman, pointing to the coffee pot.

"Fifteen maybe," Hunter replied. "Why?"

Dozer shrugged uncertainly; he lowered his voice.

"Well, the mission was a success because of what she told us," he said. "Don't you want to go thank her?"

Five minutes later, still in his combat gear, Hunter was clunking his way down a long, narrow winding passageway, approaching a very isolated part of the ship.

His destination, deep in the stern, way down on the ninth level, was the newly-christened Secure Deck 9. Originally four visitor cabins modified to make one large living area, this place now had more access restrictions than the SPOOC. Hunter passed through three heavily guarded check points on his way in—and even though he was one of the most recognizable people on the planet and he knew all the guards by name, he had his ID checked each time.

He finally found himself at the end of the cramped passageway. A sealed hatch with a heavy electronic lock awaited him. The door was painted black, a color rarely seen on any naval ship.

But oddly apropos.

He took a deep breath and then punched a four-number code into the door's lock—1-3-9-1. The hatch slid open with a whoosh.

The first thing he saw was a giant purple candle blazing away in one corner, casting flickering violet-tinged shadows all over the cabin. New Age music was playing from multiple speakers in the walls. An odd white mist hovered a few inches above the floor. The place smelled of lavender and mace.

Another breath and he stepped in. It was like stepping back in time a few hundred years. A dozen cutlasses graced one wall; a collection of feathered tri-corner hats covered another. Bandanas of all possible colors were draped with military precision across a dressing table nearby. Bottles of rum were scattered everywhere.

The pirate vibe was hard to miss. This place had everything but a parrot and a collection of wooden legs.

All of these things were the dear possessions of the person sitting in front of the roaring candle, immersed in a colorful image drawn on a small piece of light brown paper. She heard Hunter come in and quickly got to her feet.

Only then did the candlelight catch her face. Hunter felt his heart skip a beat. Raven-haired, alabaster skin, deeply green eyes glowing like emeralds. She was beyond beautiful.

Her name was Viktoria.

She was the daughter of the late Viktor Robotov.

She was also a pirate queen.

Her base was an uncharted, fog-enshrouded Caribbean island fittingly in the thick of the Bermuda Triangle. From there, her all-female gang of marine bandits mildly terrorized the Atlantic coastline for several years after the Big War. Not quite Blackbeard or even Anne Bonny, Viktoria landed there after leaving her home in Moscow at 17, the age she first realized her father was a psychopathic, narcissistic mass murderer—and that her mother was probably worse.

Things changed on her misty little island when Hawk Hunter arrived one day looking for some missing Free Canadian sailors. Though she'd held him hostage for a short while, it was only with his help that she thwarted a potentially devastating attack on her pirate base—by her own mother and her vastly superior private army.

Hunter and Viktoria parted not quite BFFs, but not enemies either. It was hard for him to have unpleasant feelings towards her. Her beauty had a lot to do with that, but it was something else too. She was the mirror opposite of her father. Her buccaneering days aside, she appeared to actually care about people, or at least about making up for some of the calamity her father had caused around the world for many years.

The first proof of this came out of the blue at the beginning of the UA's last mission. While they eventually discovered that Viktor was mass-producing nuclear weapons on an island in Tokyo Bay, it was only by an anonymous tip about the inner workings of that bomb-making factory that the UA even had a chance to destroy it. They were later astonished when they found out the tipster was Viktoria herself.

But that was just the beginning of her campaign to help the UA—and there were more surprises to come.

It was Viktoria who told them where to find the bomb on Gibraltar. In fact, she'd been working 24/7 for more than a week inside Secure Level 9, trying to locate all six of the nukes hidden by her father.

And now that number was down to five.

"You're back . . . and safe?" she said to Hunter, looking him up and down. Her voice was surprisingly sweet; her accent only vaguely Russian.

"It was right where you said it would be," he told her. "We even brought the chicken back with us."

"Well, that's good news," she said with a smile. "For the chicken, at least . . ."

She stared at him for a long moment then asked: "Do you think it's odd that this is the first time we've seen each other since I came aboard? It's been almost ten days."

Hunter stumbled for a reply. The question came out of left field.

"I'm busy, you're busy . . ." he finally blurted out. It sounded like such a classic blow-off line, even though he hadn't meant it that way.

"Well," she said. "You could at least take your helmet off . . ."

When he first met her during his adventure on her foggy island, she'd dressed in form-fitting, almost erotic pirate gear, top to bottom. It was tough and sexy. But now, she was dressed in a simple full length black gown, flowing here, tight there, plunging in all the right places, her long black hair a cascade of curls falling around her shoulders.

A sexy witch . . . he couldn't help but think.

Maybe the sexiest witch ever . . .

But it was true; he had been avoiding her, for just that reason. She was very attractive and he was very much attracted to her. But he was also smart enough to know that in the middle of special operations, those things only mix well in the movies. In real life, they turn into major complications. Keeping his distance meant preserving a bit of his sanity, if just for a little while.

She was still looking at him, though, still smiling, almost like she was reading his mind.

"Have you had your six cups of coffee this hour yet?" she asked.

His one vice . . .

"I've got one more cup to go," he told her. "But I can skip it, if . . ."

She waved him off, shaking her head no. "I think you're going to need all the caffeine you can get," she said.

"Because?"

"Because I think I've found another nuke," she replied.

Though it defied all logic, as the Gibraltar operation had just proven, Viktoria had been given a way to find the hidden nukes. This search was not based on her interpreting intercepted communications, or studying recon photos, or by reading reports from friendly spies. Nor was there any black magic involved.

It was even stranger than that.

Her secret was contained in hundreds of bits of coarse weathered paper containing scribbles made with brightly colored crayons. These scraps were roughly cut in many different shapes—squares, triangles and pentagons—and looked like pieces of a large and bizarre jigsaw puzzle.

Viktoria had received the scraps of paper in a package a few weeks before and it took her a while to realize just what they were. One summer when she was a youngster, she and her father, who was then an up and coming officer in the KGB, went on an extended tour of the Mediterranean. Her mother and siblings did not go. Father and daughter flew from place to place in a helicopter which she later assumed was owned by the KGB. Looking back on it, she realized that her father was probably on some kind of spy mission and bringing along his seven-year-old daughter provided him with superior cover.

But she also remembered being bored for most of the trip. So while her father was taking endless photographs of things, she'd used her crayons to draw pictures of all the places they visited. As soon as they returned home to Moscow, though, she put them aside and forgot all about them.

But then the mysterious package showed up, containing at least some of the old drawings, cut into the hundreds of pieces. There was also a note: "This is your chance to save the world, honey," it read. "Just don't tell your mommy."

And who was this package from?
The ghost himself, Viktor Robotov.

Viktoria contacted the UAIA in New York City soon after receiving the drawings. She told them she couldn't believe Viktor had kept them all this time, couldn't believe he'd sent them to her, albeit cut up, and somehow arranged for her to get the package only once he was deceased.

But what did it all mean?

Some of the Spooks' best analysts looked at the drawings to see if they could spot any patterns, any clues why the mad man sent them to her in the first place.

The first break came when one of the Spooks noticed that even though there were hundreds of scraps of paper, there were some noticeable differences among them. Some scraps were brown paper, others were shades of gray. By analyzing the differences they were able to put the scraps into separate piles based on everything from the thickness of the paper to the uniformity of the crayons used on them.

When these piles were complete, the Spooks were only mildly surprised that there were six of them.

Six rogue nukes.

Six drawings torn to shreds.

Save the world . . .

War of Dragons

But don't tell your mommy.

It was a very crude picture of a monkey that really cracked the case.

While many of the drawings were little more than scribbles, one piece of one drawing seemed to show a stick figure of a monkey who appeared to be looking out to sea from a great height—as seen through the eyes of a seven-year-old.

If Viktor hid six nuclear mines around the Mediterranean and there seemed to be six separate drawings and one of them showed a monkey looking out to sea from a great height—it wasn't too much of a stretch to think Gibraltar.

Now, after finding Chicken Coop bomb, they all believed that the secret to where the other nuke mines were hidden could be found in the scribbles on hundreds of pieces of scrap paper nearly 25 years old.

"Not exactly the Rosetta Stone," Dozer had said at the time.

But better than nothing.

It was almost darkly funny that even back then, Viktor was planning such diabolical madness. But for Viktoria the most mysterious thing of all was that her deranged father wanted her to save the world.

So, the extra, *extra* security on Level 9 was essential for a few reasons. One was if the knowledge of the nukes' locations fell into the hands of the wrong people, then the wrong people would be on the loose armed with nuclear weapons.

But . . . just as bad, if word got out that Viktor's daughter was now helping the UA, his sworn enemies, who knows what kind of peril she'd be in?

For all this, she had to remain invisible, in her case, to be a ghost by necessity.

She led Hunter over to her own back-lit planning table. On one side were five piles of cut-up drawings. Next to them was a drawing that had been taped back together by Viktoria with help from Spookytown. Once reassembled it was obviously a child's interpretation of a monkey sitting atop the Rock of Gibraltar.

"That was the first one," she told Hunter. "The one that brought us all here, to this place, at this moment. Once we'd put it back together, I actually had a flash of memory about the day I drew it and how that big rock looked like the biggest thing in the world to me. Until I saw this . . ."

In the middle of the planning table now was another drawing that had also been taped back together. It seemed to depict a very large dam in the middle of a desert, again through the eyes of a young child.

Hunter studied the re-assembled drawing.

"There's a dam around here?" he finally asked her.

She nodded slowly.

"Right across the strait," she replied, softly. "Just a hundred miles away."

Chapter Four

Twelve hours later, another recovery team was assembling on the deck of the *USS* USA.

It was an odd mixture of aircraft this time. When the UA captured the carrier during the Battle of New York almost three years before, their prize included 72 Su-34 Russian-designed fighter-bombers. They were big, powerful airplanes, capable of super long range and carrying a wide array of weapons as well as holding their own in air-to-air combat. Though each plane seemed to have its own peculiarities they'd had served the carrier well since falling into the UA's hands and becoming "Americanized."

But the ship also came with five operational helicopter squadrons including both the Ka-27 naval helos and big Mi-24 gunships. At the moment, six Mi-24s were at the far end of the flight deck, engines roaring, rotors turning, full of heavily-armed JAWS guys and ready to take off.

A contingent of Yak-38s was on board as well, courtesy of an allied mercenary group known as the Flying Knights of God, a modern-day aerial version of the Knights Templar. Like the vast majority of aircraft on the carrier, the Yaks were Russian-designed and built. They were also VTOL aircraft, meaning they could take off and land vertically. Though awkward in the air, the Yak-38 had been built as a fighter-interceptor, and as flown by the Knights, overcame many shortcomings due to their superior piloting skills.

Just one of the aqua-blue camouflage jets was on deck at the moment, though. Hunter was behind the controls. Once again, he was the mission commander of the recovery operation and for this one he needed something as close as he could get to a Harrier jumpjet. The borrowed Yak-38 filled the bill.

They were heading for a place called Wadi Makhzen, a huge dam in the Tangiers region of what used to be the country of Morocco. Though Viktoria had little memory of being there, after she and the guys from SPOOC painstakingly reassembled the second pile of scraps, trying to visualize the final product through the eyes of a child, it simply looked like a dam in the desert. And as it turned out, something just like that was close by. Not a hundred miles away, over the Strait of Gibraltar and in the sands of North Africa, was Wadi Makhzen.

While it was out in the middle of nowhere, Wadi Makhzen was still a dangerous place to be. As any kind of real civilization had left this part of the world a long time ago, the top of the African continent was now a kind of desert Badlands stretching three thousand miles from Morocco to the Suez Canal. Because merc groups, both good and bad, roamed the area, there really was no way of knowing who one might run into when entering the region.

No tugboats involved this time, the mission would be an armed aerial insertion. The Mi-24 Hind gunships were bristling with weapons and carrying ten special ops troopers each. Hunter's Yak would allow him to land vertically and run the mission from the ground and still be able to get airborne if any threats were detected.

And to the UA's almost miraculous good luck, at the very last minute, the Spooks had been able to contact some mercs operating near the dam, a collection of fighters who turned out to be old friends of the United Americans. The UA's overall approach would be the same: Get in, seize the weapon and then withdraw, as quietly as possible. In and out, a quick date. These fighters could prove valuable to accomplishing that goal, though for security reasons, they wouldn't know exactly what the UA had in mind until the recovery team actually touched down.

It was almost time to go.

Hunter checked with the operation's elements. The helos were fully warmed and waiting. His Yak was powered up, nozzles at a 75-degree angle and ready for his ski-jump take-off.

He did a quick visual scan of the misty deck. In the recent past, he'd experienced spectral visions out here, at night, while taking off. Ghosts? Angels? Little bit of both? They were so weird they shook him to the core every time it happened, but not in an entirely unpleasant way—as strange as that seemed. So he was always on the look-out.

Just as he was about to give the go-code for all elements to launch, he did see a blinking red light coming in his direction. His heart froze for an instant, thinking he was about to have another of his ethereal encounters.

Instead it was one of his best friends, fellow UA pilot Ben Wa, madly waving a red trouble light. He was standing just off the Yak's left wing, indicating to Hunter that he should cut his engine and talk to him.

Hunter did so and raised his canopy. The self-contained access ladder appeared and soon Ben was standing on the top step, leaning into the cockpit.

"I thought you should have this piece of intel before you take off," he told Hunter.

"Not radio-worthy?" Hunter asked.

"Maybe not," Ben replied ominously.

They were on a tight schedule, but Hunter knew his friend wouldn't hold up the party if it wasn't important.

"Did the chicken die?" he asked him.

Ben just scoffed. "C'mon, that thing's about two steps away from swimming in a stew. No, this is just plain weird . . ."

He actually looked around to make sure no one else could hear them, a funny thing to do on a flight deck that was almost shaking with noise.

"You know, back in Gibraltar," he began. "Where we just were a little while ago?"

"I can still smell the bananas," Hunter told him.

"*Banana Flambé*, maybe," Ben replied.

Hunter looked at him strangely. "What do you mean?"

Ben let out a long breath. "The Hill, the Rock," he said. "Someone cooked it good not an hour after we left. Everything from the Jews' Gate on up to the peak was torched big-time. We're hearing radio chatter from the village below. They're getting the hell out of there as quick as they can. They're saying it's all still burning. Place looks like a volcano or something."

Hunter pulled his oxygen mask off. "Damn . . . Did we miss a nuke?"

Ben shook his head emphatically. "No, apparently the Rock is still standing. It's just that the whole thing is burnt to a crisp. And that monkey problem they had? No longer a problem."

"So what happened?"

Ben could only shrug. "All we can tell is what we're hearing from the villagers on their radios," he said. "And they all seem to agree on the same two things: right before sunrise they said they saw a large winged something kind of start attacking the rock, spitting out fire and blowing up stuff.

"They also said whatever it was, was painted a very bright shade of blue . . ."

Chapter Five

Chief Zabiz-Aziz was waiting when Hunter's Yak landed.

It came straight down, coming to rest next to a high sand dune and near a small oasis. Its cloud of dust and exhaust was quickly blown away by the hot desert wind. Night had fallen by now and the stars overhead were brilliant.

Hunter emerged from the cockpit and descended the access steps. Surrounded by a dozen torch-carrying bodyguards, the chief greeted him with open arms, embracing him warmly.

Hunter and Zabiz were old friends. A couple years after the Big War ended, Hunter and the other founders of United America towed another aircraft carrier—this one without working engines—across the Atlantic, through the Med and up to the Suez Canal, all to stop Viktor from starting another global war. The floating air base concept was ultimately a success, but it was no party getting there. The slow-moving disabled carrier was a sitting duck for every rogue merc outfit in the Med who salivated over sinking an American warship.

War of Dragons

Helping to defend that carrier was a group of allied mercenaries, all experts in portable anti-aircraft systems like the Stinger. They'd turned back a number of attacks on the ship, playing a big part in the overall victory resulting from that crazy mission. If it hadn't been for them, the whole thing might have ended differently.

Those missileers had been from what was now called the Zabiz Tribe. In fact, the chief himself had been on that frightening Mediterranean cruise as a young mercenary—and he'd told many people since that it was where he learned to have courage. Though he and Hunter hadn't seen each other in years, it seemed like no time had gone by at all.

"You've aged better than me," Hunter told him. "Wish I could say the same for your threads..."

It was true. The chief's little army were all wearing desert camo combat suits that were over-used at best, rags at worst. Their weapons were also very much pre-Big War. A few were even carrying M-1 carbines used during the Second World War.

"I wish we were in better times," the chief confessed. "But the opposite is true. It has been a nightmare for us for a while. But when your people contacted me, I felt my prayers had been answered. If I can help my old friend with his problem then maybe he can help me with mine."

"That's why I'm here, brother," Hunter replied. "So, tell me your problem."

The chief didn't reply. Instead he guided Hunter up the side of the tall sand dune, warning him to stay low as they reached the peak. Then the chief indicated that Hunter should carefully look over the top.

The Wingman did so—and was stunned by what he saw.

A large valley stretched out beyond the dune and it contained a huge encampment about a half mile away. Basically a city of tents with an enormous camouflage net on top, it had paved streets, street lamps, even traffic signs. An airstrip bordered one side, outlined in blue runway lights. And there were lots of weapons about, including several large collections of Russian T-62 tanks.

Oddest of all maybe was that everyone Hunter could see was wearing a bright silver combat helmet. This made little sense, as silver was not a color you wanted to wear in any form while in combat.

Hunter counted the tents and quickly did the math. The numbers told him this was a bivouac for at least ten thousand soldiers, maybe more. And the place was giving off a seriously bad vibe. His psychic insides were short-circuiting; the evil here could be cut with a knife.

The chief crawled up next to him.

"Who are these mooks?" Hunter asked him.

"We call them the Philistines," the chief replied. "They are from what used to be called Lebanon. They are horrible people. They have no hearts. No souls. No consciences. They believe any crazy idea that comes along and they don't appreciate anything. And who wears a silver helmet?"

"They're a long way from home," Hunter said. "So these people have been bothering you?"

"They've been *killing* us," the chief told him. "They are devils straight from Hell."

They both slid back down the sand dune to where the chief's bodyguards had hidden Hunter's Yak under some palm fronds.

"We had our base nearby," the chief continued to explain. "And they showed up out of the blue one day about a year ago, captured twenty of our men, beat them, tortured them and then interrogated them, trying to get information about some long lost treasure that was supposedly buried somewhere out here.

"We fought back and rescued our guys. But we had to abandon our little home and become a guerilla army. Our tribe had two hundred members before these bastards came. Now we are down to less than fifty."

"That all took great courage," Hunter told him. "For you and your men . . ."

The chief looked him over for a long moment and said: "But why do I have a feeling you're here for the same reason? To find this treasure?"

Hunter let out a long, slow breath. Time to come clean.

" 'Treasure' is an odd way to describe it, my friend," he began. "But yes, we are looking for something that was hidden in this area just about a year ago. And believe me, while this might be a whole new twist to this, it could be what these guys are looking for too."

"So where do we come in?" the chief asked.

Hunter patted his old friend on the back.

"If you can get us to the Makhzen Wadi Dam," he said, "we hope to start looking for it there . . ."

Hunter hesitated for a moment then added: "Unless you already know where it is . . ."

The chief smiled, displaying a mouth full of gold-filled teeth.

"I do not," he said. "But I might have a good idea . . ."

The Mi-24 Hind gunships landed in perfect formation, a line of six, one touching down after the other.

The JAWS troopers inside jumped out and, as always first priority, established a defensive perimeter around the landing zone, which now held the gunships, Hunter's

Yak and ten heavily armed Toyota trucks operated by the Zabiz tribe.

Once the LZ was set, Hunter sought out Captain Cook and had him climb the side of the sand dune with him.

The JAWS CO took one look over the top, saw the huge, camouflaged camp and whistled softly.

"Let me guess," he said. "Those are all bad guys . . ."

"It's a pretty big army to be camped way out here," Hunter told him. "And the chief says not only are they complete a-holes, they're looking for a 'buried treasure' and have been since they arrived about a year ago. So the question is: are they looking for the same thing we are?"

"But if they are, how did they find out about it?" Cook wondered. "I thought we were the only ones . . ."

"They had to have been tipped off somehow," Hunter said, grimly. "Not to the exact location, though. Otherwise they wouldn't be beating on these poor people."

Chief Zabiz was suddenly beside them.

"The time is right," he told them. "And we are ready to go."

Possibly the most insidious part of Viktor's plan from the grave was that the six nuclear-armed mines he left behind were thought to be disguised as normal, everyday things like oil drums, trash cans, manhole covers, even chicken-coops.

In other words, they could be hidden anywhere in plain sight.

The mine they recovered from Gibraltar was circular and about the size of an automobile tire. It weighed about 80 pounds and had a blast equivalent of 3.5 kilotons, or eight million pounds of explosive. A marvel of microcircuitry and creative wiring, it was an extremely compact weapon, armed with a radio controlled timer that was still ticking down when they managed to disable it back on the carrier.

Would they find the same kind of thing here?

Or would they find anything at all?

All of the UA aircraft were put under camouflage netting next to the small oasis. Then a combined recovery team—JAWS troopers and Zabiz's fighters—struck out north along the bottom of the giant sand dune.

Hunter, Cook and the chief were in the lead. About 20 feet in front of them, Hunter saw a figure in a long white robe and hood, face hidden, quasi-religious symbols chained around their neck. They were carrying a lantern which was giving off the barest of light, but still showing them the way.

They walked for about five minutes before starting up a steep hill covered with sand brush and thick olive trees. A barely discernible path led to the top. It was strange because Hunter suddenly noticed a change in the air. No longer arid and dusty, now there was moisture in the wind.

They reached the top of the hill to find themselves looking down on an enormous dam. It seemed to stretch out into infinity. Hunter saw the hooded guide simply point to the walkway that ran along the very top of the dam wall and then disappear into the night.

"This is the Wadi Makhzen," the chief told them. "Also known as the Tangiers Dam. Before the Big War, the Moroccan government really knew how to collect water. They spent billions to build this dam and several more. They run all in a line right to the sea. But there is something very odd about this place."

Hunter studied the gigantic structure through his NightVision goggles. It seemed at least as big as the Hoover Dam back in the states and, due to its sheer size and extremely isolated desert location, was a bona fide engineering miracle. But he saw nothing unusual about it—at least not at first.

Cook had come to the same conclusion. The long narrow walkway, three feet wide at most, that ran along the top lip of the massive dam looked like it went on for miles. There was a bunch of pipes running alongside it and halfway across, appearing very small at the moment, was a fire hydrant. But that was it.

Was this really the place Viktoria had visited years before?

"Lots of water," Hunter said, still missing something that to Chief Zabiz seemed obvious.

"*Tons* of water, my friend," Zabiz told him. "And lots of concrete. Tons of water and concrete, but nothing that can burn. So, why would you need a fire hydrant way out there?"

Five minutes later, Hunter, Cook and two JAWS engineers were making their way across the narrow walkway atop the lip of the dam.

It proved to be a very windy journey, even more so than during the Gibraltar operation, not even 24 hours before. Hunter and the engineers were carrying cutting tools, Cook was carrying the radio detection device they called The Boop. But they all needed to hold onto the wire railing on either side of the walkway for fear of being blown away.

The Boop started buzzing about a hundred feet before they reached the fire hydrant. Approaching it very carefully, looking for trip wires or some other kind of hidden security devices along the way, they discovered the hydrant wasn't even a hydrant. It was not connected to anything, there were no pipes running in or out of it, no valves or couplings that they could see. Most telling, there was no firehose nearby.

"And not a chicken in sight, either," Cook said, moving the Boop around the hydrant and hearing it loudly whine in response.

But then, a big problem. The bomb was the same size as the Gibraltar weapon, tire-shaped and painted black. But unlike that bomb, which at 80 pounds they'd been able to lift out and carry away, this one was actually *bolted* into the base of the fake hydrant, a dozen large screws holding it in place.

As mission commander, Hunter had to make a decision: take the time to unscrew all the bolts or just cut out the whole damn hydrant, heavy as it might be, and take it with them somehow. He went to put his hand on the top of it, just to see if it was made of real cast iron—because if so, he estimated it would probably weigh at least 500 pounds meaning they would need one of the helicopters to lift it out.

But the second he touched it, he was hit by a sharp electrical shock accompanied by an explosion of sparks. He was knocked backwards and swore loudly. The sparks alone surprised the hell out of the rest of the team.

They immediately went to one knee, weapons up and ready in the howling gale.

"It's hooked up to something," Cook yelled to Hunter over the wind. "Probably not a security device because you'd be fried by now. Maybe a heater?"

"Would you need a heater for one of these things out in the middle of the desert?' Hunter yelled back, not knowing the answer. Cook shrugged as well. "I know it gets cold out here sometimes, but does it get *that* cold?"

Hunter examined the hydrant and its base through his NightVision goggles, being careful not to touch the thing again. He couldn't see any electrical wires at all, but that was no big mystery. Any wiring could be internal. But Cook had been right: had it been a security device, the voltage probably would have killed him. So, a short-circuited heater, hidden away somewhere?

Maybe . . .

Hunter stood up, gritted his teeth—and touched the hydrant again.

Nothing . . .
Again.
Still nothing
One more time . . .
Nothing.

"That's weird," Cook shouted to him, now touching the hydrant all over for himself. "It's suddenly harmless."

"I know," Hunter replied. "But why do I feel like I just flipped a switch?"

Not a moment later, his radio began buzzing.

It was Clancy Miller, the JAWS XO, back at the LZ base camp.

His first words were stark. "Hawk—something might be heading your way . . ."

"Something?" Hunter replied.

"Yes, something airborne, coming in from the north," he reported. "Real big but flying very low. It's covered in smoke, like it's on fire or something, so we can't see what kind of plane it is. But it's really moving—and going by us . . . right now . . ."

This was followed by much static and the sound of something flying above Clancy's position.

Hunter and the others heard it for themselves a few moments later. A low growl combined with a high whistling noise. Everyone on the top of the dam turned in its direction and saw an incredible sight.

It was an aircraft, yes, a big one—and yes, it did appear as if it was on fire, or better put, smoking very heavily, which was weird because, though it was hard to tell in the dark, it seemed to be flying straight and true and not to be in any distress.

"What the fuck is this thing?" Cook breathed. They were all stunned by it. Hunter had never seen anything like it before.

Suddenly its nose lit up—and now it looked like nothing less than a flying, fire-breathing dragon. It went by them, fast and low, the flames shooting from its nose creating a blinding orb of bright light around the front of the aircraft. An absolute deluge of ordnance was pouring out of it and it was only that the walkway was so narrow and the beast was shooting at them from an extreme angle that UA team wasn't vaporized in an instant. None of them could believe they were still alive.

Once past them, they could hear the smoking aircraft turning around high above the desert floor. Seconds later, the scream of its engines told them it was coming back.

Hunter didn't even think about it. Whatever this thing was, taking apart the hydrant to get at the bomb was no longer an option. Carrying the hydrant out whole was not possible either.

So he just yelled: "Plan B!"

On those words, the team began running back across the narrow walkway, withdrawing from their position with all due haste.

The air dragon completed its turn and was just lining up its nose with the top of the dam when the team reached the end of the walkway, diving into the foliage at the peak of the olive grove hill. Hunter and Cook were the last to reach cover.

The winged giant went over them a moment later, the streams of flames and smoke coming out of its nose looking almost exactly like a long tongue of fire coming from the mouth of a mythical aerial beast. Next thing they knew it was gone, disappearing into the night. But a few seconds later they could hear it starting to turn around yet again.

"Goddamn," Cook breathed. "This is too weird."

"Weirder than a chicken sitting on a nuclear bomb, yes," Hunter replied. "But I think I'm the reason it showed up, whatever it is. I think that shock I got up there tripped something and summoned that thing. Maybe there was a similar device hidden in the chicken coop that night..."

"Well, it's not like we can go back and check," Cook said dryly. "Not since the Big Rock was turned into a big charcoal briquette."

Hunter thought a few moments, then asked Cook: "Are we doing anything tomorrow night?"

"Not that I know of," the JAWS CO replied.

Hunter made another quick decision. "OK," he said. "Let's come back tomorrow night."

On those words, the team rose out of the bushes as one and started double-timing it back to the LZ.

They reached the encampment and quickly began preparing to take off. During the entire sprint back, Hunter's mind was working overtime on this latest unexpected twist. He knew there had to be some connection between the bomb and the frightening airplane. But what?

All of the UA aircraft were ready to go when the masked aircraft suddenly reappeared for a third time. It was coming from the north, its nose and now wings absolutely blinding with tracer rounds pouring out of them. It zoomed over the LZ, though seemingly not interested in them. Instead it trained its sights on the hidden tent city on the other side of the giant sand dune.

The UA soldiers and the Zabiz bodyguards scrambled to the top of the dune to see a horrifying sight. The mystery aircraft was absolutely tearing up the Philistines camp. Its powerful on-board weapons were obliterating the tents and everything around them, carving up the base like a gigantic flaming scythe.

"Lucky they were the bad guys," Cook whispered to Hunter as they watched the terrifying air assault.

Hunter just looked at the others and said: "Time to go . . ."

They ran back down the dune and jumped into their aircraft. The choppers all took off at once, carrying both the JAWS guys and the Zabiz fighters, including the chief. Hunter was the last to go. The mystery airplane was coming right at him again just as he was taking off; it was heading back towards the burning Philistines encampment, nose aflame, looking for more people to kill.

Hunter was almost mesmerized by this thing. It was so expertly covered in smoke and the darkness even he still couldn't tell what kind of aircraft it was.

So, he let it roar over him and then pointed his nose up and hit his gun camera, allowing him to take a brief video of the beast.

Chapter Six

The recovery team returned to the carrier empty handed, but at least intact.

It was raining heavily when they arrived; a squall had blown up just as they came within sight of the big ship. The sudden downpour soaked the vast flight deck. Then the wind began to blow.

The Mi-24 gunships came in first. They were all over their safe weight limit because they were hauling back the JAWS guys plus the remaining members of the Zabiz Tribe. The deck crews helped the newcomers out of the rain and down to the portside galley where a temporary sick bay had been set up.

Only once the copters were taken below did Hunter finally land, coming down vertically on the drenched and pitching deck.

Ben was waiting for him in the spray. They dislodged the video module from the nose of the Yak, wrapping it in their jackets to keep it from getting wet. Then they hustled over to the shelter of the main deck hatchway and finally got out of the elements.

Hunter shook the rain from his flight suit, at the same time telling Ben what occurred back at the dam including, in vivid detail, their encounter with what Chief Zabiz called the *hasha wa*— roughly translated: "the air beast" —and the nearly impossible destruction it could sow. Ben listened, jaw agape.

"Was it painted bright blue?" he finally asked Hunter.

"It could have been painted like a zebra for all we got to see of it," Hunter replied. "All I can say is it's a large airframe, it has a freaking scary camouflage thing going on and it's hauling a lot of weapons. I've just never seen anything like it; a big airplane pimped out like a fighter bomber or something."

That was quite an admission for him. He was the most famous pilot who'd ever lived, known in every corner of the globe. He'd been involved in more battles than he could remember and thought he'd seen every airplane model that still existed. But it was true: he'd never seen anything like what was flying around the Tangiers Dam. Whatever the hell it was.

"Let's go down to the TV studio and have Tony 3 look at this video," Ben suggested. "He has filters and enhancers. I'm sure he can get a clear shot of whatever it is . . ."

"I've got to 'coffee-up,' first," Hunter told him. "I'll meet you there."

The starboard galley was deserted, a rare moment in the never-ending hustle and bustle of the big ship.

But the staff knew Hunter would be stopping by, so they left a pot of coffee warming on the stove. He happily scooped it up and grabbed a mug.

At that moment, his special sense of ESP kicked in. Just a voice, somewhere deep in his brain telling: *turn around, someone is watching you.*

He did as advised and saw he was no longer alone in the mess hall.

Sitting in the last seat at the table furthest away from him, was a figure dressed all in white, hood up and covering their face.

This was not a member of the crew. It looked like Zabiz's guide, the one who led them up to the dam. Hunter hadn't seen them get on the copters back at the LZ, nor getting off the ship on their return. Yet, here they were.

Hunter took an entire cup of sugar—that was essential—and walked out to the mess hall to see if he could be of some help.

But by the time he got there, the figure was gone.

*****

It turned out to be a long walk to Tony 3's studio.

Hunter slowly realized he'd just seen a ghost. He was sure of it because he'd seen more than a few ghosts in his life and one in particular for the past couple years. He wasn't sure why these hauntings happened to him, but they did and to him it was as real as breathing or blinking your eyes. He'd had a few universe-hopping adventures over the years and always thought they made him more susceptible and perhaps just more accepting of seeing visitors from somewhere else.

But he always felt very weird whenever it happened. And he was feeling very weird right now.

He reached the tiny TV studio to find Ben already poring over the video footage from the Yak's gun camera.

Tony 3 was with him. A usually-jovial bowling ball of a man, his real name was Anthony Antonio Antonioni and he was the carrier's combat media guy. He'd been associated with the UA since the so-called Freedom Express adventure, when Hunter and his allies drove the first train to cross the United States after the Big War ended and America was still in its most fractured state. It was a little step in a long journey that eventually ended with the country being made whole again—and Tony had been there with them for the long haul.

Ben dragged a chair over for Hunter.

"Are you ready for this?" he asked as Hunter sat down.

Still shaky from his ethereal encounter, Hunter could only reply honestly.

No, I'm not," he admitted, pouring out and draining a cup of coffee, "But let's do it anyway."

Tony started twisting knobs and pushing buttons on his large video control panel. His big wall-mounted TV came to life.

"I was able to filter out some of the smoke," he explained. "Not a lot. But I think it's enough for you to ID the plane . . ."

"Good to hear," Hunter said, trying to sound confident as he poured a second cup.

Ben smiled and patted his friend on the shoulder. "OK, but we mean it," he said. "You better strap in for this."

Tony 3 started the huge VCR and a dark, smoky image quickly appeared on the TV screen.

It showed the air monster going over Hunter's Yak and then disappearing into the night. The video was just five seconds long and even that much was extremely difficult to see because of the blinding weapons flash coming from the plane's nose.

"Just as I remember it," Hunter said, draining cup number two.

Tony punched more buttons and put the video into a loop. Every time it came around again, he engaged more video filters, taking away layers of what he called distorting interference. By the time the loop had played ten times, a lot of the smoke and flash was gone.

And what remained was maybe more improbable than Hunter had ever expected.

The mystery airplane was a highly modified C-130 Hercules cargo plane, one of the most ubiquitous airplanes ever. Designed by Lockheed back in the 1950s, literally thousands had been built in the years before the Big War, and more than a few could still be found these days.

But nothing like this.

It appeared to have four massive guns sticking out of its nose. The flare from these weapons was what gave it the appearance of a dragon spouting fire. The plane also had multiple weapons embedded in its wings, similar to World War II fighter planes. The difference was old fighter planes would have a maximum of four wing-mounted machine guns. This plane had six large cannons sticking out of *each* wing. A full half dozen on either side.

But that was not all. A large turret had been added just behind the cockpit and it was holding a quad-fifty, meaning four .50-caliber heavy machine guns that all fired at once. This only added to the already incredible destruction the plane could bring from the sky.

It was no wonder the air monster could flatten the huge Philistines' encampment with just a few horrible, deadly passes. The recovery team had been lucky to get out of the area alive.

Still, they were left scratching their heads about three things.

"Do we think this is the same airplane that tore up the Rock at Gibraltar?" Hunter asked, pouring out one last cup of coffee.

Ben and Tony 3 just shook their heads.

"The plane over Gibraltar was described as bright blue," Ben said. "This one looks bright red."

There was no disagreement there. Even with all the filtering it was clear the plane was painted in almost dazzling crimson.

"Could someone completely re-paint an airplane like that in just twelve hours?" Tony wondered.

"I'd have to say that's unlikely," Ben said.

So what was going on then? Why were these strange aircraft shooting up territory and people in the first place? It would be too much of a coincidence for this to be happening in the same two places near where the nuke mines were secretly located. That meant, on two occasions now, similar aircraft had been seen during the mine recovery operations or shortly thereafter. But who was flying them and under whose orders?

Puzzle number two: Why did this aerial monster attack the Philistine army? True, the world was a lot better off without them—but their only crime in this case was looking for the bomb in the first place. So why did they pay such a sudden and unexpected price?

And finally, a question that was asked before and was the most unnerving of the three: why were the Philistines suddenly so interested in looking for the weapon in the first place? They had to have been tipped off—but by whom? In theory, the only person on Earth who knew all aspects of Viktor's plot from beyond the grave was his daughter, Viktoria—and she was in the safest safe house possible, hidden away deep inside the gigantic USS *USA*, surrounded by three layers of guards.

There was no way she could have physically gotten word out to anybody, let alone an army of trash heads like the Philistines, and besides, why would she?

So how did they know?

Hunter didn't want any more coffee.

At this point, he just needed to get to his bunk and fall asleep for the first time in nearly four days. He didn't need ESP to know it would be a while before he had this chance again.

When they'd first envisioned this mission, they felt it would be dicey, but do-able. Very quietly find the six nuke mines, take them out of circulation and deal with any bumps along the way. But now a cascade of bumps had descended on them, ones that could turn into mountains very quickly. The scorching of Gibraltar, the air monster over Tangiers Dam, the reason the since-dispatched Philistines were looking for the same treasure as they?

Get some sleep, he'd heard a voice say, *before things get even worse....*

So, he returned to his cabin, cleaned up and then went horizontal on his bunk, finally ready to crash.

Not thirty seconds later, a knock came on his cabin door and someone slipped in.

He thought he was already in a dream. He looked up to see this gorgeous face looking down at him, a kind of mist enveloping them in the strangest way. It took him a moment to recognize her.

It was his ex, Dominique—and she was holding a pot of steaming coffee . . .

"You've got to hear what I just heard," she whispered urgently, handing him the coffee pot. "So pour a cup and let's go."

Dominique was no longer the demure, alluring femme fatale of years past.

Gone was the luxuriously long and flowing blonde hair. It was now short, neat and attractive, those golden locks barely touching her shoulders. Gone too was the long black slinky dress and the spikey high-heel leather boots. By her own wishes, she was now a full-fledged Spookytown Spook, working directly for UAIA Command these days and in more than just her usual undercover role. For this, her new job, she dressed the part. A very tight pair of combat utilities, blue combat boots, hair tied back and tucked up under a baseball cap and mirrored sunglasses.

Lean and mean—but no surprise, also uber-sexy.

It was a bit awkward as Hunter hastily got dressed, gulping coffee as he did so. Considering their past, and some intimacy recently coming back into their old relationship, these days he wasn't always sure how he should approach her. He would always love her and their many adventures, some of them otherworldly, could never be forgotten.

But in this world, in this reality, she was just as involved in the intelligence-gathering aspect of this mission as he was in the recovery part.

So at the moment, she was all business.

They were soon down on Security Level 9.

Dominique breezed through the checkpoints, while the guards still insisted on checking Hunter's ID.

"You don't have to enjoy it so much," he told the third group after they cleared him to pass.

As it turned out, Dominique had been visiting Secure 9 a lot lately. Her overall assignment for the recovery missions was to help Viktoria unravel the mystery of the drawings. It was a smart choice. Dominique had always been very intuitive—and a little psychic, too. Most important, she had patience, which was mandatory when looking for clues and solving riddles.

What Hunter didn't know was that Dominique and Viktoria had become very close since working together. As soon as her door whooshed open and he and Dominique stepped inside, the two of them were in an embrace, even though Dominique had been down here just twenty minutes before, the time it took her to get the coffee, collect Hunter and walk back.

Finally, Viktoria turned her attention to him.

As always, she looked him up and down and said: "Two times in less than one day? One of us is getting lucky."

As Hunter was trying to decode this, Viktoria took him by the arm and pulled him over to her lighted planning table.

It now had three more re-created drawings displayed on it, bright crayon masterpieces laid out with multiple murderboard-type strings connecting them. But the image being projected up through the table was not a huge map of the Strait of Gibraltar, but of the entire Mediterranean.

"We think we are zeroing in on where three more of the bombs are," she told him, excitement in her emerald eyes. "That's the good news."

"And the bad?" he asked.

She looked at Dominique, who gently eased Hunter into the nearest chair. She took the coffee pot from him and poured him another cup.

"Follow closely," she said. "It's not as complicated as it first sounds."

Only slightly insulted, Hunter studied the lighted map of the Med. Viktoria leaned in close to his right side; Dominique did the same on his left.

Viktoria began to explain: "All this time we were assuming my father planted these mines at places that would make them hard to find. Difficult but random places. But now we might have found a pattern of sorts, that where they were hidden was part of an even larger scheme and not random at all.

Hunter swigged his coffee. "I'm with you so far . . ."

Viktoria pointed to the Strait of Gibraltar.

"Imagine if the first mine had gone off," she said. "It would have resulted in a significant amount of debris. At 3.5 kilotons, I'd say approximately 96,000 tons of it would have fallen into the strait. Not enough to block it. Unless . . ."

"Unless?"

"Unless the Tangiers bomb had gone off as well," she replied. "That dam is sitting on a mini-fault line, which basically connects two larger fault lines. If the dam bomb goes off, it would create an earthquake that would have deposited another 90,000 tons of debris into the strait and together, that would have blocked it permanently."

Hunter shook his head, his spirits beginning to plunge. He drained his coffee and poured himself another.

Viktoria went on: "If this happened, in hours if not minutes, coastal regions all around the Mediterranean would be inundated by massive flooding caused by the Med water not being able to get out to the Atlantic. Water levels would rise 20-30 feet in a matter of days. There'd be tidal waves maybe hundreds of feet high. Any ships in the Med and Aegean Seas would be washed away immediately. Major coastal cities would suddenly be underwater. The human losses would be cataclysmic.

"But then, almost as quickly, the water levels would drop drastically because the large volume of water that usually moves from the Atlantic Ocean into the Mediterranean would also be blocked."

She sidled up even closer to him if that was possible and said: "Now imagine if some of the other bombs are located in places that, if detonated, could seal off the Med entirely, completely and forever. What do you think would happen then?"

"Nothing good, I'm sure," he replied.

"In a very short time, the Med would dry up and turn into a bed of salt miles thick," she explained soberly. "This in turn would create a gigantic solar reflector, spiking the Earth's temperatures. The change would be quick, uncontrollable and more than enough to melt the polar ice caps in days.

"If that happened, Europe as we know it would be gone forever. At least half will be under water. Beachfront property in Switzerland. Across the Atlantic, Hudson Bay probably overflows and several hundred trillion gallons of water will head south, washing out a big part of Canada and very likely going through the middle of the U.S. until it reached the Gulf of Mexico. It might even be a big enough event that it creates a new inland sea somewhere between Chicago and New Orleans."

"Viktor was a genius," Dominique said to him with a shrug. "He was demented, but he knew what he was doing when he dreamed up all this. I mean, like in death he could get what he wanted for so long in life: ultimate power over the planet by destroying it . . ."

"Let's say you're right," Hunter told them. "Then where do you think the other mines are?"

"I'm not sure exactly at the moment," Viktoria replied. "But I'm looking into a few places to start."

She pointed to the upper northwest edge of the map. "Something that affects the flow of water into the Med from rivers coming out of the Alps," she said.

Then she moved her finger across Europe to the opposite side of the map. "Maybe something around the area of the Black Sea as well," she went on. "I'm working on putting together more drawings to see if any match this new idea. But we have to remember that no matter what, even if just one of these bombs goes off in just the right place under the right conditions, it will still lead to catastrophic consequences."

Hunter glanced at Dominique. She looked deeply upset, not the usual state of affairs for her. The planet had been torn apart by wars big and small since World War III, but short of another global nuclear war, the Earth itself was never really in danger—until now.

"But how do you know all this stuff?' Hunter finally asked.

"Well, you can thank my father for that, too," Viktoria replied. "When I was just 12 years old, he sent me to the Moscow Institute of Geology to study rocks. It was a punishment for me doing something bad, but I actually liked it and stayed there until I ran away from home at seventeen."

Hunter looked at her as if to say: Really? But instead he said, "That's very impressive."

"And it isn't really much of a stretch," she went on. "The Med dried up five million years ago and stayed that way for 170,000 years—and that affected everything around the world for hundreds of thousands of years after that."

They were all quiet for a few moments, taking in and digesting all this bad news. Hunter really didn't want to bring up the next subject, but if not now, when?

He finally told them about the air monster they'd encountered over Tangiers and how a similar aircraft was seen burning the Rock of Gibraltar just hours after they'd retrieved the nuke mine there.

He turned to Viktoria. "Have you ever heard of such an airplane?" he asked. "Did your father ever mention anything like it?"

She thought for a moment. She was not a novice. She knew what a C-130 was and could appreciate the terror one could bring if tricked out with weapons the way Hunter said it was.

But she had to shake her head.

"Dear old dad was not a big fan of airplanes," she revealed. "Maybe that's why he hated you so much. You were everything he wasn't and knew he would never be. But I can't recall hearing or seeing anything like you've described. And believe me, I would have remembered."

Dominique shook her head, a little despondently now. Again not like her.

"Why is it always like this?" she groaned. "Why are we always fighting the clock? Or some kind of crazy airplane or out of this world ship? Why do we always find ourselves in these impossible situations? With always mountains and mountains to climb before we can get anywhere?"

Hunter had no answer to that—and he felt it too. Ever since the Big War, he and his crew had faced nothing but major struggles trying to put America back together and, once it was re-united, keeping it that way.

Oddly, it was Viktoria who spoke up. "Want the opinion of an outsider?" she asked.

Hunter just nodded.

"Oh my God, would I," Dominique breathed.

"There's a simple reason for it all," the pirate queen said. "You face down these problems, you beat the clock, you get over all those mountains because you have reasons to—you love your country. You love the planet. That's why—and that's why you overcome them."

Hunter and Dominique were speechless; neither knew what to say.

Viktoria recognized their discomfort and smiled.

"Take it from me," she said with a wink, pushing back her long raven hair. "Even your enemies admire you."

Chapter Seven

The plan was nearly the same as the night before.

The six Mi-24 gunship helicopters set down next to the Makhzen Wadi dune, on the same LZ as 24 hours earlier.

Five were full of JAWS special operators; the sixth was carrying a dozen fighters from the Zabiz tribe, including the ex-missileer himself, Chief Zabiz. They were wearing new combat suits and headgear equipped with NightVision, and were armed with Banana 16s, oversized M-16s complete with huge banana clips, a signature of all UA forces.

The combined team assembled next to the oasis. They could see hundreds of vultures overhead, circling the devastated Philistines' camp on the other side of the dune, a grim reminder of what happened the previous night. Everyone on the mission shared the same opinion of the blinding horror the Philistines suffered not a day ago.

Better them than us . . .

The recovery team split into two groups. Ten men would camouflage the aircraft and protect the LZ. The others would trudge back up to the Tangiers Dam hoping to do what they hadn't been able to the night before.

Captain Cook was in the lead. It was darker tonight and even windier. They could hear strange howling noises around them and every few seconds the sky would crackle with heat lightning. They walked along the bottom of the big dune for ten minutes and eventually found the tall hill covered with olive trees. Up they went, the troopers feeling the increased moisture with every step, the result of all that water in the middle of the desert.

They finally reached the end of the path and here was the dam again. It looked a lot larger tonight and more dangerous. The wind was blowing wildly up here and the howling noises only got louder. Add in the lightning and it was already like a bad horror movie.

"I didn't think it could get any weirder than last night," Cook whispered to Chief Zabiz. "I was wrong . . ."

They now faced the very narrow walkway running across the lip of the gigantic dam. Cook checked that the direct recovery team—three of his men, three Zabiz fighters—was ready to go. He gave them a hand signal and together they quickly began making their way across the precarious walkway atop the mile-high structure.

None of the problems they'd faced out here the night before had changed. Unlike the chicken coop bomb, this mine was crazily secured to the base of the hydrant by many very large screws. The question they'd pondered over the last 24 hours was simple: when the time came, what was the best way to get it unattached?

The *quickest* way would have been to pack a little plastic explosive around each screw and let it rip. However, using explosives around nuclear weapons was usually not recommended. The screws would have to be removed by hand with the largest wrench they could find on the USS *USA*. But that would be an hours-long job under the best of circumstances. The vertigo-inducing height and the very high winds would only add to the challenge.

So, it was good that the team was not here at the moment to snatch the nuclear mine. Instead, they were here to activate it.

They reached the hydrant and confirmed nothing was different from the night before. Now it was all up to Cook. He took a deep breath, steeled himself, and then touched the top of the hydrant. He was immediately zapped with 5,000 volts.

Knocked back about a foot, he swore fiercely into the vicious gale, which had somehow doubled in ferocity. He steadied himself, took in a deep breath, then said: "Major Hunter owes me a year of free drinks for that . . ."

Then an unnerving vibe enveloped them. They really *were* out in the middle of nowhere. Seemingly miles above the ground with the only sign of civilization being a bunch of red blinking lights way out on the horizon, probably the city of Tangier. No matter, there was nothing in between but the stark desert darkness and the ungodly swirling winds. When all was said and done, for tonight's new plan to work, the recovery team had to play the part of bait.

That was never more obvious than now as the team crouched down and began to wait.

One minute.

Two . . .

Three . . .

Finally Cook's radio buzzed to life.

It was Clancy Miller, the JAWS XO, back at the LZ.

Just like before, his words came over as direct but anxious.

He said: "Here it comes again . . ."

The air monster roared over the dam just seconds later.

Coming out of the north as it had the night before, it was once again flying low and trailing great amounts of smoke. The team had already taken cover as best they could on the narrow walkway. Still the turbulence left in the big plane's wake almost knocked the raiders into the abyss below. As it was two of the Zabiz fighters nearly went over the side, only to be caught by their JAWS colleagues at the last possible moment.

Cook helped pull one of his guys back who in turn had his hand on a Zabiz fighter. That's when Cook got a brief glimpse of the bizarre airplane. Even through the clouds of smoke now he could see it was definitely painted bright red—almost sparkling red. And definitely not blue.

"Son of a bitch," he swore again. "There *is* more than one of them."

Out over the water now, the plane went into a shaky turn, suddenly firing its guns everywhere and nowhere. The sudden pyrotechnic display was loud and wild, like thousands of fireworks being shot all over the night sky.

"It's having a tantrum," Cook heard himself say out loud, "Like a little kid, having a fit."

The team got to its feet and started racing to the safety of the olive tree hill. But running along something that was a mile high and seemed just a little wider than a tightrope, in now very, *very* high winds, was going to be very difficult. Just a few seconds in, it already felt like they were running in place.

And by that time, the air monster had completed its screeching, frightening turn—and was coming back.

*****

The members of the back-up team waiting atop the olive tree hill were in the best position to see what happened next.

The huge airplane, wings now whistling strangely, had turned 180 degrees and pointed its nose back towards the dam. Leveling out at just 500 feet, and with another screech, it booted its engines to full throttle, causing its artificial smokescreen to magically double in size. Incredibly the all-encompassing dark gray fog was moving right along with the hurtling air monster, leaving a long contrail of dirty exhaust behind.

This masking job, the massive guns in its nose, the multiple cannons on its wings and forward turret, and now the Stuka-like wing-mounted whistles that produced a blood-curdling screech with every increase in speed. Everything about this plane was meant to frighten—and at the moment, it was doing a great job of it.

The most disturbing noise of all—a kind of echoing banshee scream—actually came when the beast slowed down a bit, its engines shrieking in protest. But it was necessary. It had spotted the direct recovery team, still battling the wind and trying to get off the walkway.

But at the moment time was against them.

And everybody knew it.

The beast opened up with all its guns, wings screeching again, sending a wobbly fusillade of all kinds of deadly ordnance in the direction of the American-Zabiz team. Suddenly the dead of night was lit up bright as day.

Hellfire . . .

For real . . .

But then . . . another sound, another great flash, another ear-splitting sonic concussion buffeted by the great winds.

And suddenly it was there, streaking by the nose of the air beast.

Cranked arrow shape, painted red, white & blue, all guns and flash and speed, it looked like a visitor from another world, a weird sci-fi world.

It was the F-16XL Cranked Arrow.

Behind the controls, Hawk Hunter, aka the Wingman.

What followed next was an exercise in bending the laws of aerodynamics to a most extreme degree.

Actually the super-jet appeared a split second before the aerial monster opened up on the recovery team.

It arrived just in time to affect the air currents in front of the big plane and cause its deadly barrage to go awry. Disrupting the air flow in front of such a big plane could prove disastrous for it, especially when it was flying at barely 500 feet. Needing to avoid a deadly stall, it suddenly pulled up into such an extreme climb, no pilot in their right mind would have ever attempted it.

Yet, Hunter yanked back on his own controls, just missed pancaking on the desert water and started following the big plane up.

The beast reached 5,000 feet before it pulled out of its screaming climb. Then it attempted to bank right, but Hunter had already flashed by that wing, once again disrupting the air currents, and making it impossible to complete the maneuver. The big plane staggered in the air for a moment, almost as if its controllers weren't sure what to do.

The XL did not hesitate though. It went up and over the huge gunship just as it was returning once again to level flight. With the big plane's attention now distracted, the direct recovery team resumed its dash across the top of the dam, finally diving into the cover of the olive tree groves below.

The big plane turned again, going up on its left wing, as if it was intending to fly right at the XL head-on. But there was little chance of that. Hunter sent a two second burst of tracer fire from the six-pack of M-61 cannons in his jet's nose right across the air monster's snout.

Once again, in response to the danger, the plane abruptly increased power and went into another screaming climb, only to have Hunter rocket by its nose a second time, and in the process breaking the sound barrier with an ear splitting *boom!*

Clearly tiring of this game, the big plane went back up on its right wing and began a long slow turn away from the top of the dam, away from the strange battle.

And at that point, the XL chose not to follow.

Instead, it went straight up on its tail and disappeared into the night.

Chapter Eight

The sun rose exactly four hours and nineteen minutes later.

The first beam of light lit up the top of the mammoth Tangiers Dam, reflected off the faux fire hydrant and bounced to a mirror on the far side of the Wadi Makhzen, which in turn activated a solar powered battery atop el-Aziz Mountain five miles away.

Itself nearly a mile high, the mountain's peak held wires that wound their way down to its center where a massive man-made cave was located.

With this first spark of light, a control panel on one wall of the cave lit up. This in turn activated a small electrical generator next to the panel. As soon as this generator warmed up, it turned on a power bus and the electrical system of the large airplane sitting in the middle of the cave came to life.

It performed a series of self-diagnostic tests; the lights on the control panel blinking green whenever a check was complete. A soft whirring started up inside the airplane itself—its large bank of batteries waking up and recharging themselves. This took two minutes and then the air beast settled down into what was called stand-by non-emergency power.

This was how it spent many of its days: warmed up and ready to fly when called upon.

It had been out earlier in the night, the second time in as many nights it had been called on to do a mission.

Just from a wear and tear point of view, it would be beneficial for all concerned if this state of standby limbo today lasted for a few hours at least, if not a few days.

But that was not to be.

Thirty minutes after that first ray of sunshine hit the top of the hydrant five miles away, the airplane suddenly came to life again in a burst of emergency power. Something was wrong out there. It had to go back out and try to fix it.

Its four engines started simultaneously, the resulting smoke and exhaust being quickly filtered out of the massive chamber. One minute later the engines were warm enough for flight.

There was one more quick systems check then, with all in readiness, the massive doors to the vast cavern opened.

But instead of the plane's forward looking cameras seeing its short take off runway in front of it, they found instead a line of soldiers blocking its way. Many were pointing their weapons at the plane's cockpit; others were holding large spotlights and directing them onto the bulbous nose of the airplane. The plane began moving forward a couple times, but just an inch or two before stopping, uncertain what to do next.

Finally the electric eyes on the end of its nose couldn't process so much incoming light all at once. The plane's flight controls blinked and then just shut down. A moment later the engines died too, and the four propellers stopped turning. Suddenly it was very quiet inside the cavern.

The soldiers waited a moment, just to see if it was real.

Then they let out a spontaneous cheer. The best way to capture a dragon was when it was still in its lair.

That's what the United Americans had just done.

Back on top of the Tangiers dam, a smaller recovery team radioed the cavern to say they'd removed the hydrant and thus the nuclear mine, unscrewing it from its base, cutting the radio wires to its transmitter and then lifting it out with one of the carrier's Ka-27 helicopters.

Two down, four to go . . .

Back in the cavern Hunter and the others celebrated the good news with a massive display of fist bumps.

Then they inspected the strange airplane they'd just seized.

Trapping it here had been based on one of Hunter's wildest ideas, that the air beast wasn't all it appeared to be. The way it flew, the way it reacted to hostile action. He thought the key might be engaging it at the height of one of its "tantrums," literally confusing it in flight. Then instead of shooting it down, he simply followed it home.

Landing in the gigantic mid-mountain air strip, spinning around on its moving floor, its nose pointed front once more, the winged beast waited to be called on again. That call came when the smaller dawn-busting team on top of the dam touched the hydrant a third time, set off the alarm and summoning the air monster to action.

Until it was stopped here.

Hunter's wild idea turned out to be right. The airplane had no crew. It was remote-controlled by radio, a sure sign of Viktor's hand. Like the Russian-built robots on their aircraft carrier, the members of Solomons Cult they'd fought a few months before and the killer drones that put an end to the Asian Mercenary Cult Army even before that, the air monster was radio controlled, working off orders programmed into it years before, and revived by radio transmissions from somewhere else, possibly a network connecting the other bombs.

When needed, the plane came alive and defended the site of the nuke mine, or more accurately put on such a frightening display no one wanted anything to do with it.

Sleeping sentinels—just like real dragons.

The Americans' inspection of the plane's exterior revealed the heavily-modified C-130 was indeed a gigantic fighter plane, armed with massive weapons and a large cargo bay to carry lots of ammunition.

Its smoke screen came from a device that spit oil onto the hot parts of its engines, and then funneled the resulting smoke to seven outlets located around the plane. It was also equipped with JATO bottles for crazy short landings and take-offs. This was how it operated in and out of the mountain base. These were pretty impressive modifications, especially since the whole thing was indeed remote-controlled or better put "self-controlled."

But it was the inside of the plane that really knocked them out. Four gigantic GAU guns were sticking out of its nose. Just one of these massive Gatling type weapons, as carried by the famous A-10 ground attack plane, could destroy an entire squadron of tanks in a matter of minutes. Four of the huge guns firing at once seemed almost unthinkable.

The plane also carried an array of six 50mm Viper cannons embedded in each wing, and the quad-fifty in the forward mounted turret. Just like the World War II warplanes it was based on, the air beast's battle strategy was basically point and shoot with everything it had and whatever happens next happens.

The recovery team walked the length of the gunship several times, captivated by the weaponry it contained. They had no idea who built it for Viktor. But everything inside was made in the USA before the Big War.

"The world has thousands of arms dealers," Cook said after taking it all in. "But ninety percent of them are morons. Whoever put this together knew what they were doing."

Hunter looked around the airplane's interior one more time as well.

Then he said: "Well, it's ours now . . ."

Chapter Nine

The bridge of the USS *USA* was very busy at the moment.

Sitting high atop the skyscraper-like superstructure, glass windows looking out in almost every direction, it was from here and the primary flight bridge directly below, that the chief operations of the carrier were run.

They were still in the Atlantic, now about twenty miles off the coast of Morocco, fifty miles south of Gibraltar. It was late afternoon and the weather was turning bad again.

Up on the bridge's forward window, Dozer, Ben and JT were looking out into the stormy skies. The weather had turned around 1200 hours and had steadily deteriorated ever since. With barely an hour of daylight left, concern on the bridge grew.

"I *really* don't like this," JT was saying, and not for the first time. He was scanning the horizon with high powered binoculars. "The idea is just too *out there* . . ."

"Did you try to talk him out of it?" Ben asked, never taking his eyes off his own binoculars.

JT just shook his head. "Yeah, right . . ."

Dozer was on an open-line to the carrier's meteorology room. The seas were getting very choppy and the wind was gusting up to 30 knots. He wanted the weather people to tell him improvements were on the way. But instead they told him the atmospherics were actually getting worse.

"Oh good," Dozer said dryly, back to scanning the horizon again. "That will just add to the fun . . ."

They spotted him about eight miles out, an array of blinking lights helping them see through the thick dark clouds.

Word had gotten around the ship about what was supposed to happen, so anyone who could spare the time, showed up on the superstructure's balconies or on the walkways surrounding the enormous flight deck. Others watched on the ship's closed circuit TV system.

No one wanted to miss it:

Hunter was going to attempt to land the big C-130 super gunship on the carrier.

It had been done before. Way back in 1963, the old U.S. Navy was desperate for ways to supply its aircraft carriers when they were in the mid-Atlantic or mid-Indian Ocean, places far out of range for their normal supply planes.

Someone suggested they try to land a C-130 cargo plane on a carrier, just to see if it would work—and to just about everyone's surprise, it did.

This would be different, though. True, the USS *USA* was the largest warship in the world, actually the largest warship ever built, and while its flight deck was wide enough to accommodate the gunship's 132-foot wingspan, unlike an American-built carrier, the *USA* had an enormous ski-jump on its bow to help the ship's VTOL aircraft get a fuel-saving rolling start.

How do you land a large airplane on a ship sporting something like that when it was probably going to take the entire deck for any safe stop? And how are you going to do it without having an arresting hook to catch the flight deck's landing wires?

This was what the entire carrier was talking about. The Wingman was rarely wrong about anything, and almost infallible in aeronautical matters like this.

But could he really do the near-impossible?

They were about to find out.

The air beast was over the ship a few minutes later.

Wings wagging through stormy skies, it seemed enormous and over-sized as it flew by, down around 1,000 feet.

Yes, it was totally Hunter's idea to carry their prize back to the carrier and maybe get it to work for them. But he'd have to get it aboard first. That's why he requested he make this flight alone.

It was on his third loop around the ship when he finally called the bridge.

"I've got it figured out," he told Dozer. "But there's one thing you've got to do for me, please . . ."

The USS *USA* had been sailing due east at 30 knots heading into the wind when Hunter arrived overhead. Ten minutes later, it had taken the sharpest turn its propulsion gear would allow and was now heading in the opposite direction, due west, sailing with the wind.

The bad weather hadn't changed. With increasingly choppy seas and fading daylight, the betting was that Hunter would simply get the big plane down to its slowest possible flight speed and then using his brilliant piloting skills and fancy work on the engines and brakes bring the gunship in safely and in one piece.

But no . . .

The way he did it turned out to be nothing short of spectacular.

JATO stood for Jet-Assisted Take-Off.

They were basically military grade bottle rockets attached to the bottom of large airplanes to significantly shorten the length of runway needed to get airborne. Ignite anywhere from four to six of these bottles and the aircraft was literally rocketed into the air.

But employed in an even more unconventional way, JATO bottles could be used for shorter than usual landings. The key was to have them fire facing forward, to cushion the blow of slamming down for a landing with little or no landing roll-out. This too had been tested by the U.S. military back in the 80s—this time with questionable results.

But that didn't mean Hunter wasn't going to try.

As it turned out, it was all over very quickly.

Hunter brought the enormous gunship over the carrier one more time, turning violently on its left wing to bleed off energy and to line up the nose into the wind and onto the "backwards" sailing carrier.

But then instead of coming in for what would be considered a normal carrier landing, he activated the plane's forward facing JATO bottles and in an explosion of white and yellow flames, came nearly straight down and hit the deck with an enormous bounce—and that was it.

Those that saw it couldn't believe their eyes. Suddenly the huge C-130 gunship was sitting on the deck of the *USA*.

The resulting spray of smoke and exhaust hung over the odd airplane for nearly a minute after it arrived in such an unusual fashion. Hunter meanwhile simply dropped out of the plane and came out of the steam and smoke like some conquering angel.

The deck crew who came forward to retrieve his flight gear, in awe of what they'd just seen, reported that he thanked them for their help and then said: "I need a cup of coffee . . ."

Chapter Ten

Hunter headed for the starboard galley, hoping the cooks had left a pot brewing for him and wondering if any ghosts had long since gone.

He found Dozer waiting in the kitchen for him instead. He already had the pot and a large, over-sized cup.

"You're getting this to go," he told Hunter, handing it all to Hunter. "You've got to hear what the Spooks came up with . . ."

They went down to the SPOOC. Passing through the strict security, they found two techs inside poring over the two nuclear mines the UA had recovered.

"They're not fakes, are they?" Hunter asked them.

"We're not that lucky," one tech replied.

Both mines were sitting on a temporary workbench set up inside the ultra-secret planning room. They looked like landmines from World War One, just on steroids. About the size of an automobile tire, both had handfuls of wires running in and out of holes in their black steel case. They looked dangerously crude.

It had taken the Spooks a while to dismantle the Gibraltar mine once it had been recovered. In doing so, they were unpleasantly surprised to discover a tiny digital clock hidden underneath the bomb's trigger. It was ticking down to a date in the near future: May Day, the biggest holiday in the old Soviet Union.

In other words, the mine was actually a time bomb.

The Spooks determined all this while the recovery team was in the midst of its second trip to the Tangiers Dam. Once that bomb was brought aboard and the Spooks detached it from the fake fire hydrant, they disassembled it like the first and found another counter, right where the first one was.

It too was a time bomb—but it was ticking down to a time 72 hours *earlier* than the Gibraltar bomb.

"So Viktor wanted them to go off at staged times?" Hunter asked. "Three day intervals?"

"It might not be that simple," one tech explained. "We did a time forensics analysis on them. There's a chance that as soon as the Gibraltar bomb was deactivated, the Tangiers Bomb started ticking faster."

Hunter needed a moment to process this.

"You're saying there's a kind of fail-safe system built-in that if any of the nuke mines were shut down, the countdown for the others would speed up?" he asked.

The two techs and Dozer nodded at the same time.

"That could be the case," Dozer said. "They both have tiny radio transmitters and receivers in them, essentially telling them what to do. If we assume they're all equipped like these two, then there's a chance that if any of the radio signals from any of the bombs is altered or shut down, it hastens the countdown on the rest of them."

It was all too clear to Hunter now. "So, Viktor wanted his daughter to 'save the world' but do it while a clock was ticking."

Neither Dozer nor the techs could disagree.

"Cataclysmic ecological disaster?" Dozer said. "Ticking time bombs. Remote controlled air dragons flying around? Viktor's still pulling the strings. Even from the grave."

Hunter checked the date on his flight watch.

May Day was just one week away.

Chapter Eleven

They held the crew assembly out on the deck.

It was the next morning. The rain had cleared away and the sun had reappeared. The ship's command had an important message for the crew. Bull Dozer decided it was best they all gather in the same place, shoulder to shoulder and hear the news.

Not wanting to address the ship's company from high up on the super structure, instead Dozer climbed onto the wing of one of their Americanized Su-34 jet fighters. After making sure that he could be heard via his bullhorn, he laid it all out—everything they knew about the mines, where they think they could be hidden, the diabolical aspect to *where* they were hidden and how the ramifications might include flooding a large part of America if even one of them went off, never mind four. He also revealed that Viktor's daughter herself was helping them in the recovery efforts.

The crew stood silent and sober-faced as a sudden fog enveloped the ship. It was the first time for many hearing the details about the calamitous situation they found themselves in.

Dozer let it all sink in then explained that to save the world, including their beloved homeland, from absolute irreversible damage, they would have to sail the length of the Mediterranean and find the four other bombs. The problem, he explained, was if they were too late and any of the four remaining nukes went off, then some kind of catastrophic event inside the Med itself would be inevitable.

Not mincing his words, Dozer explained that if this happened, the ship could be hit by a tsunami more than 100 feet tall, something even the massive carrier could never ride out. But as Dozer emphasized, if they didn't do anything, that catastrophe was going to happen anyway.

He gave each crew member a choice: leave the carrier and stay on dry land until whatever was going to happen was over. Or try to save the planet from Viktor's insanity beyond the grave.

But no one wanted to stay behind.

Take care of this problem now—and maybe the world won't end? Maybe there would be no beachfront property in Paris—or Fargo, North Dakota?

No brainer really.

The assembly concluded on a sincere patriotic note; a display of love of country that was not shouted at the top of the lungs or grunted from the depths of a full stomach.

It was more of a loud whisper than anything, a hushed response from a congregation one might hear in church.

"USA . . ." those assembled said all together, almost as if they were praying.

The ship's company was dismissed soon afterwards.

And then the *USA* turned east, sailed through the Strait of Gibraltar and into the Med, quickly disappearing into the mist.

PART TWO

Chapter Twelve

Batu Khan woke up in a small grove of trees atop a high hill looking out over a huge dry valley.

It was the dead of night. He was lying on his back, a warm wind blowing over him. He wiped his eyes to see billions of stars staring down at him. The air smelled of lavender, thyme and . . . disinfectant.

It was almost peaceful in a way—except Kahn had no idea how he'd gotten here.

The last thing he remembered was being at a celebratory feast for his army, the Abax Zong, which in ancient Mongolian meant Army of Revenge. The festivities had taken place in Bucharest, a city that Khan's 50,000-man army had just captured after two months of fighting. He recalled lots of nasty whiskey and potent drugs being passed around and meeting a gorgeous Russian escort named Minky and then going outside with her to do some pure Merck cocaine.

The next thing he knew, he was here.

Wherever here was.

Five other figures were sprawled on the ground nearby. One was his personal bodyguard Tuk. He was lying out cold just a few feet away.

"Useless bastard," Khan thought out loud.

He kicked Tuk awake and urgently pointed to the others lying nearby. They were stirring now as well. As groggy as he was, Tuk had to be ready to do his job.

Khan was a direct descendant of the infamous Mongol warrior, Genghis Khan—or at least that's what he liked to tell people. His army was currently overrunning the Balkans in what was already a two-year campaign west. Just about all of southern Europe was lawless and up for grabs these days and, just like a handful of other marauding armies in the area, Khan the warlord was looking to take over a sizable piece.

In this respect he was a very important person. So he had to be protected at all costs.

Tuk was finally up on his feet and standing over him by the time the four others had awoken. To Khan's groggy astonishment, he recognized two of them.

One was Gunnar Sven-Sven, a completely loony warlord from Scandinavia who imagined himself just as much a descendant of Leif Erikson as Khan was of Genghis Khan. His army had driven as far south as Rome and now controlled a large part of Italy. They'd come into contact with Khan's forces on a few occasions along the way causing some minor skirmishes. This led to an unwritten agreement between the two that they would try to stay out of each other's way while rampaging through various countrysides.

But they were hardly friends. Khan was a small man, shaved head, tattoos, wiry but strong and a superb horseman. Sven-Sven was nearly seven feet tall and three hundred pounds at least. He never went anywhere without his axe, and yes, he had it with him now.

He looked as perplexed as Khan about how he'd wound up on top of this hill, among the trees with all those stars overhead. He too had been transported here with his bodyguard, an absolutely enormous Viking even bigger than Gunnar himself.

The two remaining individuals were just now getting to their feet. One also appeared to be a bodyguard of sorts; they just had a certain look about them. Heavily scarred, missing a few digits or perhaps an eye. Always huge, always scary looking.

But it was the last man to stand up who was the most frightening of all.

Khan recognized him immediately; the others did too. He felt his heart sink to his boots.

"This is all we need," he heard Sven-Sven mutter.

It was Crazy Norman . . .

In an age where many warlords wanted to be celebrities as well, harkening back to their supposedly long lost bloodthirsty relatives, Norman made no such pretenses.

He didn't need to. He *was* a barbarian, a savage. Brutal. Inhuman. Almost as big as Gunnar, but dressed like the black knight of the roundtable, he was all these things and more. And so were the men in his 65,000-man army, best known simply as the Goths.

As an example of their butchery, Crazy Norman's army had attacked the city of Caen in France during one of his raids into southern Europe. Quickly overcoming the city's defenses, for the next three days, his men raped and killed anyone they could find. Then they ransacked the city—and left. So horrendous those 72 hours had been, it took another two full days for those who'd been hiding from it all to finally come out of their attics and basements and see the daylight again—at which time the Goth Army unexpectedly returned and raped and killed all of them as well.

Khan was no shrinking violet and neither was Gunnar but Crazy Norman was a psychopath. He got off on being cruel. The thousands of butchered bodies he'd left in his wake were testament to that.

Trying to shake his headache away, Crazy Norman loudly announced: "I don't care which one of you two is responsible for bringing me here. You have both taken your last breaths."

Then he nodded to his goony bodyguard and pointed to Khan.

"Kill him first," he said.

The man produced a Gurkha-like short sword and began advancing on Khan. Tuk took up his rightful position, blocking the way, but he quickly realized he was not going to beat this freak at anything. Protecting his boss would be just a formality now, before they were both sliced to death.

Over . . . what?

What the hell were they even doing here?

The grisly double killing was averted a moment later in the most unusual way. Just as Norman's man was about to raise his sword to strike Tuk, the blade suddenly went flying across the grove, an ear-splitting whip crack echoing in its wake.

Then the night was lit up by a hundred points of light. They were coming from behind the trees, surrounding the six now-totally confused men.

Out from these shadows came a woman dressed all in black leather, with knee high boots, a massively-plunging bodice and a long flowing black cape.

She was holding a bull whip in her hands, rolling it back up and putting it on her sexy utility belt all in one smooth move. Behind her, also dressed in black, were several dozen soldiers, each carrying an AK-47 assault rifle equipped with a pinpoint laser aiming device.

"Do you know who I am?" she asked the six astonished men.

They did—and even Crazy Norman started shaking with fear.

It was the woman they called the *Chernya Vdova,* the Black Widow, or more simply *Vdova*, wife of the late Lucifer-incarnate himself, Viktor Robotov.

She saw their fear and smiled, enjoying the moment.

Then she said: "Relax, ladies. If I wanted to kill you, you'd already be dead."

Chapter Thirteen

More chloroform followed and the next time Khan regained consciousness, he was sure he was on a large warship.

He'd woken up in an expansive cabin. Dark gray walls and floors, lots of wires and wire busses overhead, two hatchways to get in and out and rivets running everywhere. He could feel a gentle rocking as if they were docked somewhere.

He wasn't wrong. He *was* aboard a large warship—but this warship could fly.

It was called an Ekranoplan. It was the size of a typical naval cruiser but looked more like a large jet bomber with its pointed nose, large wing and high tail. Two smaller wings up near the cockpit held eight jet engines whose downward thrust allowed this vessel to cruise a few feet above the water, similar to how a hovercraft operated.

Ekranoplans could carry a variety of highly destructive weapons, hundreds of troops and could move across the water at speeds in excess of 350 M.P.H. The Soviet Union built a number of these monsters before the Big War and more than a few survived or had been rebuilt.

The strange contraptions were the war machines of choice for the Widow Robotov.

She too had her own army and it was larger and better equipped than those of her three guests. She and her warriors were well known for riding around the world in a squadron of Ekranoplans, terrorizing innocent populations, robbing and sacking entire coastal cities and generally creating misery for people already made miserable in the aftermath of the Big War.

That she'd engineered the recent events in Tokyo Harbor which led to the UA nuking the place was now accepted as fact in the post-Big War's dark criminal underworld. Terrorists, drug lords, tin-pot dictators and many of the world's marauding armies were now beginning to accept that, based on what they knew happened in Tokyo, the *Chernya Vdova* had taken her late husband's place to become the world's leading super-villain, the first woman to claim that piece of infamy.

Khan was well aware of this, as were his equally dopey counterparts, Crazy Norman and Gunnar Sven-Sven. They too were in this cabin with him, just now regaining consciousness with their goons at their side.

They'd been placed in chairs scattered about the room. A squad of the Widow's special ops soldiers lined the walls and the exits, watching them. They were a collection of giants rivaling the size of Crazy Norman himself. With their jet black body armor, oversized helmets, opaque face shields and AK-47 assault rifles, even Norman seemed to shrink away from them.

The Evil Queen herself suddenly swept in the room, surrounded by more of her over-sized bodyguards.

"Commanders—to the planning table," she said with a thick air of authority. "Button men, remain seated in the back."

Under the watchful eye of the Widow's goons, Khan, Gunnar and Crazy Norman took their places at the planning table dominating the middle of the room. A small closed-circuit TV was at one end displaying a screen full of white static. A closed paper file, obviously thick with 8x10 photographs, was placed beside it, along with a bottle of vodka and a single glass.

"Allow me to get right to the point," she said, her voice dripping with distain as she poured out some vodka for herself. "Before my husband died, he hid a half-dozen nuclear devices around the Mediterranean. I would like to retrieve as many of them as possible and I'd like you to help me do it."

The three men were stunned speechless. They thought sure they were here to get whacked, Widow-style.

It was just as she assumed. She went on: "And simply put, which ever one of you helps me reach my goal first, I will pay you one thousand pounds in gold."

The three men were still without words, but now for a different reason. The currency of choice in the post-war world was silver, as in bags of silver. But gold was even more precious than before the Big War. Receiving one thousand pounds *in gold* would set up anyone for life. Such an amount would equal a startling $200 million in pure bullion.

"Do you know where these bombs are?" Sven-Sven now asked excitedly.

The Widow looked at the faux-Viking like a butcher looks at the next chicken to go. But she kept it together.

"If I knew where they were, my friend, why in all hell would I need you?" she asked him sternly.

"But how do you expect to find them if they are hidden?" Khan asked her. "Do you have any clues?"

She reached over and switched on the small portable TV set. It cleared of static to show a room somewhere inside the flying battleship. It held dozens of women, all of them chained to mess tables, sorting through thousands of pieces of shiny black and white paper with varying degrees of smudges on them.

"We have a bit of a puzzle on our hands," the Widow explained, showing them crude photocopies of what to them looked like the scribbles of a young child. "We found these among my late husband's effects. We're sure that clues to the bombs' locations can be found in those pieces of paper. That's not the problem. Our friends down there are sorting them and we'll figure out that part eventually. The bigger problem is this: The United Americans are also looking for these weapons. Their carrier just came into the Med and they may have already found two of them."

Now a nervous silence came over the room—even Crazy Norman was uneasy on hearing the Americans were close by.

"For my plan to work," she went on, "and for you to have a chance to get the gold, we have to neutralize that aircraft carrier."

Khan spoke up now. "I hope you're not suggesting we try an armed landing on that ship. Because we know the Tokyo Yakuza gang tried that and they didn't get within ten feet of the deck. It's not a ship; it's literally a floating moving fortress."

"The Yakuza were fools," she replied softly but tersely. "They went in dicks first and wound up as food for the fishes . . ."

She smiled evilly and then added: "I have a better idea . . ."

"Such as?" Gunnar asked.

"Let's look at another group my husband was associated with," she replied. "They were a bunch of losers called Yellow Star. Sad really, because they had a good thing going in the South Pacific until my husband got involved and as usual turned it into a crap storm."

"Why do you admire them, then?" Khan asked.

"Because when they tried a mass attack on that carrier, they nearly succeeded," she replied. "They did it with drones and it was only a last moment radio glitch that prevented them from success."

"What are drones?" Crazy Norman asked sincerely. He really didn't know. None of them did exactly.

"Again, that shouldn't concern you," she quickly told him. "This is what should concern you."

She showed them a picture from the photo folder. It was of a warehouse jam-packed with large wooden crates.

"Ever hear of Silkworm missiles?" she asked them.

They had. The Silkworm was a Chinese-made blunder-buss of an anti-ship missile, popular in pre Big War times. It was nothing like the French Exocet or the Russian-made P-800 Oniks as far as accuracy or elaborate technology, but it did have a 1,000-pound high explosive war head, three times larger than the Exocet.

One Silkworm in the right place could do serious damage to a major warship like a cruiser. How many it would take to sink a carrier was unknown. How many would it take to sink the USS *USA*? Also unknown.

But this photo showed hundreds of them.

"Impressive," Khan said. "But what does this have to do with us? We have armies, not navies."

"I know that," she snapped. "But I also know all three of you have contacts with pirate groups operating in the Med. Isn't that true?"

It was. Because the three warlord armies operated close to the sea they relied on pirates as a major part of their on-going re-supply. In fact, since the three armies converged on southern Europe about a year ago, some pirate groups were making more money moving cargo for them than they had from their pirating activities.

The Black Widow went on: "If you supply them with these missiles and if that carrier is sunk, whoever pirate group did the sinking will get the gold. Simple as that."

The three warlords were really all ears now. Hire-out some doped-up pirates to take on the Americans? And if their plan succeeded, a thousand pounds of gold would be theirs? Could there ever be a nicer deal?

But there was still something strange about all this.

"Why don't you just deal with the pirates directly?" Sven-Sven asked her.

For the slightest moment all the vitriol seemed to run out of her. Eyes down, she said: "Because I prefer not to deal directly with them. I've had some experiences with pirates in the past that just didn't end well."

An hour later, after yet another round of chloroforming, the three warlords and their bodyguards were airlifted back to the top of the leafy hill next to the dry valley.

They were all very groggy by now, and even though awake, they were mostly sitting still trying to get the woozy haze and their brutal headaches to go away.

A note pinned to Crazy Norman's tunic told them to wait there until other transportation arrived to take them their separate ways.

In anxious anticipation of that, each bodyguard took his boss to a far opposite edge of the hill, putting as much distance between them as possible. Their trip to Widow's flying battleship had not been a bonding experience for them. In fact, it would be pure luck if all of them were still alive when that promised transportation finally showed up. Tuk got Khan situated near the eastern edge of the hill and in the best defensible position he could find. He urged the boss to try to get some sleep, as he would stay awake and defend him to the death.

Khan laughed at him. "That just means I'll die in my sleep," he said harshly.

But a moment later, he took Tuk's advice, stretched out on the ground and was asleep in less than a minute.

Finally Tuk got to sit back and close his own eyes. Like the others, he had a splitting headache from the three rounds of chloroform with maybe another on the way. Still, it already seemed like a dream to him.

They had no idea where they were at the moment, where this hill was. They had no idea where the Widow's Ekranoplan had been docked. In the foggy aftermath of being repeatedly knocked out in just a few hours' time, everything had an air of unreality to it.

At some point Tuk fell asleep himself—and had the strangest dream.

Or at least he thought it was a dream.

He was gazing out on the large empty valley before them and heard a bizarre noise coming his way. Suddenly a tiny airplane appeared from nowhere. It was flying not 100 feet away from him out over the hill.

It stopped in midair, its engine spewing flames and smoke. Someone inside looked out at him for a moment.

Then there was an explosion of bright light and the strange little airplane disappeared in a flash.

Chapter Fourteen

The pair of Ka-27 helicopters appeared out of the south, arriving over the target area at just about dusk.

The lead copter was piloted by a UA veteran nicknamed Phil Cobra. He was one half of the famous Cobra Brothers helicopter team. His "brother" Don was right behind him, trying his best to keep a tight formation despite the blustery and howling winds around them.

The Brothers usually flew the fierce and frightening UH-1 Cobra attack copter, thus their well-known nicknames. That was not the case here, though. The KA-27 was not an attack helicopter; it was designed to hunt submarines. But they were far away from any water at the moment. At least the unfrozen kind.

Slowly filling their cockpit windscreens was the massive Alpine mountain known as the Matterhorn. It was more than 15,000 feet high, rising three miles over the border of what used to be Switzerland and Italy. And it was nearly symmetrical, it had four sheer sides and they aligned almost perfectly with the points of the compass.

There was magnificence to it, no doubt, but it was also an extremely treacherous place. Before the Big War, nearly five hundred people had died trying to climb it.

More than a few more had lost their lives trying to get to the summit by other means, namely helicopters. The main reason was not just the deadly, non-stop high winds. It was that these winds could come from any direction, at any time, and shift again within seconds. The mountain's pyramid-like shape was always blamed for this. But over the years, centuries even, many people had become convinced this strangely aligned mountain was either haunted, cursed or both.

At its base was the Matterhorn glacier, part of the much larger Zmutt Glacier. Together they contained almost seven square miles of solid ice. The Cobra Brothers had seen the numbers: if a nuclear weapon went off anywhere near this place, all that ice would instantly turn into about 120 *billion* gallons of water and, with nature taking its course, it would head south at high speed, in the form of a 50-foot tidal wave, a half mile wide or more. It would destroy everything in its path, all the way down to the Mediterranean, more than 150 miles away.

Once all that water reached the Med, it would contribute even more to the already catastrophic coastal flooding that would be ongoing if any of the other nuke mines went off.

But . . . the debris resulting from the blast would also wind up blocking one of the major sources of water flowing into the Med: the run-off from the Alps. Without that, and other similar sources, the Mediterranean might even dry up quicker than anticipated.

That's why the Cobra Brothers were here.

To help prevent all that from happening.

Now about ten miles away from the dangerous peak, each Cobra referred to a crude photocopy of a reconstructed child's drawing taped to their control panel. It was the result of many hours of work by Viktoria, Dominique and the Spooks, fitting the puzzle pieces of yet another drawing back together. While it was there for comparison purposes, looking at the drawing now, though obviously seen through the eyes of a child, it was almost eerie how much it looked like the perilous peak.

They were both emotionally tied to the drawing. In the pre-mission briefing, they'd witnessed the extraordinary scene of Viktor's daughter breaking down when talking about the picture. Between tears she'd said: "I can't believe it. We flew by that thing in a helicopter and I remember asking him way back then, what would happen if it all melted?"

With these thoughts running through their minds, both pilots reached the same conclusion: This was definitely the place.

Don Cobra went in first. He circled the peak and then yelled to the six JAWS troops riding in the back that it was time to mount up. Each man hitched his gear, pulled down his goggles then put on an oxygen mask. They called ahead that they were ready to go.

Now came the tricky part.

Don Cobra brought the copter so close to the top of the Matterhorn, its nose actually became embedded in some ice near its peak. Taking their cue, the six troopers jumped to the snow below, with Jim Cook in the lead, carrying the Boop.

Its LED light began glowing red the instant he hit the ground. For that one moment they all just hunkered down against the ferocious rotor downwash combined with the incredibly high winds and waited for the helicopter to back away. Then, once they could see clearly, they began looking for places this mine might be hidden.

The peak wasn't completely snow-covered. The winds were so bad, they blew away a lot of the snow at the very top. So it was actually rocky up here, with lots of ice.

Cook began waving the Boop in front of him. Between its LED's glow and its buzzing sound, he was able to get it to point him toward a large cascade of ice, frozen in place eons ago while falling from one of the many ledges around them. It looked like a freeze frame of a water fall.

"Who wants the honor?" Cook asked his guys, trying to be heard above the winds.

The job fell to his XO, Clancy Miller. He scrambled over to the natural ice sculpture, and with one mighty swing, hit it with the butt of his rifle.

There was a great crash and a million little ice particles exploded into the gale. They quickly turned into a frozen mist and blew away. What remained was a bright red, old-fashioned London-style phone box right out of Dr. Who.

The entire team advanced now. Surrounding the box, the troopers could actually hear the Boop buzzing over the roar of the ever-changing winds.

Being careful not to touch it quite yet, Cook looked in the phone box's door window and saw a tiny vent coming up from the floor emitting a small but steady stream of warm air.

Each man in the team had a look. "It must have been a bitch to drill all the way down through the Matterhorn until you hit something thermal below," Cook told them. "But it sure beats the chicken-method."

Just like the hydrant on the Tangiers Dam, this bomb was connected to the bottom of the phone box by twelve massive bolts. But the arrangement came with an added complication: the bottom of the phone box was sunk inside a giant bucket of frozen concrete buried in the snow.

No matter. The Americans had come prepared.

This time, they brought a blow torch.

But there was something they had to do first. Already freezing, wind blowing so hard he was losing his hearing in air so thin they all needed oxygen masks, Cook nevertheless let out a groan and yelled: "This is the part I *really* hate . . ."

He took a pair of thick rubber gloves from his utility belt and managed to put them on.

Then he clenched his teeth and touched the side of the phone box. There was an immediate crack of electricity as a bolt of static ran down his arm, down his leg and into his combat boot.

Cook was thrown back and started sliding towards the edge of the 15,000-foot high peak. Three of his men jumped at the same time, stopping him before he reached the precipice.

"That's it," he roared, getting back to his feet. "Hawk buys for me until doomsday!"

He thought a moment and then added: "Whenever that might be."

It took four minutes to cut through the bolts and another three to lift the phone box en masse up and out of the cement bucket.

In the meantime, Phil Cobra had brought his copter around and the team began to attach the box to the cargo hook dangling beneath the aircraft. That's when they heard a terrifying yet familiar sound. Above the wind. Above the racket of two helicopters flying in very cold air.

Cook had mini headphones on—and he heard it louder than anybody. That same mechanical scream. Nothing changed it. The desert heat, the bitter cold. It still sounded the same, like Death itself was coming for you.

The troopers knew that speed was vital now, so they finished attaching the call box to the copter winch and gave Phil the thumbs up. Just as the copter was pulling away, the air monster arrived on the scene.

This one was painted in orange so bright, that even through its smokescreen it looked like it could melt the perpetually frozen landscape of the Alps.

"Not very subtle is it?" Cook asked dryly as the plane quickly approached.

The beast let out a long growl, something the Americans knew now was the noise of all of its weapons being armed. This meant the plane was just seconds away from opening fire on them.

But it never got that chance.

Because in the millisecond before the big plane's firepower was unleashed, another sound started echoing through the famous mountains. Another mechanical scream, coming out of the sky, way overhead. The recovery team all looked up to see the same type of big C-130, bristling with the same type of weapons, diving towards them at nightmarish speed.

In the end it was simply quicker firing its weapons than the big orange plane. The diving air beast opened up with its four giant Gatling guns and with a perfect shot to its mid-fuselage, tore the orange plane in two in less than a second. It then broke into four separate pieces, falling towards the snowy ground, long streams of smoke, steam and fire following them down. It all finally crashed into the Vispa River, three miles below.

And that was it. That's all it took to gun down the monster gunship charged with protecting the Matterhorn bomb.

It was not a fair fight—but that's the way it went in dogfighting, no matter how big the planes were. It was a pilot's skill more than anything else that usually won the day.

Triumphant, the second monster plane did a wide loop around the peak and then flew directly over the jagged mountain, wildly wagging its wings. Those on the peak gave it a mock salute as it roared by.

Yes, it was the exact same kind of airplane that now lay burning in the Vispa River below.

There were only two differences. One, Hawk Hunter was behind the controls of the victorious airplane, and two, that plane was wearing a very hastily applied paint job, that just happened to be red, white and blue.

Chapter Fifteen

The deck crew on the USS *USA* was literally battening down the ship's hatches when the Matterhorn recovery team began to arrive home.

The ship was waiting for them about 50 miles off the old Italian city of Genoa. It was two hours past sunset, but the huge carrier was lit up like daytime. They were in the midst of an NBC alert. Standing for nuclear, biological or chemical attack, everything that could be sealed, shut down or locked up was done so. The rest of the carrier's air fleet was below decks and the crew was at their battle stations.

Most unusual, massive bags of water lined both sides of the deck, all the way up to the ski jump and back. Actually huge internal fuel bladders used by the carrier's tanker planes and now filled with sea water, they were also stacked high all around the carrier's giant superstructure, making it look like a fort in the Old West, expecting an attack.

It was true—the ship's command staff *was* expecting an attack of sorts. But it would not be in the NBC realm; much more likely it would be a massive tidal wave if and when any of Viktor's remaining nukes went off. The water-bagging was a Russian recommendation, put in place when they first built the mammoth ship. Knowing it was crucial to maintain the center of gravity during something as extreme as a tsunami, the old Russian operations logs claimed that heavy water bags would help keep the large ship stabilized in such a situation by balancing out the flight deck.

It seemed highly unlikely to have any effect, but, Dozer asked for it to be done anyway. If they were going to face a 100-foot tidal wave he wanted to have all precautions in place—even ones the Russians recommended.

*****

Phil Cobra's Ka-27 came in first, lowering the battered phone box directly onto the huge flight elevator, allowing the device to be brought below and secured in a vault with the rest of the ship's nuclear materials. That made three nukes recovered and three to go. At that moment the countdown to May Day was six days and sixteen hours. But there was a feeling on board that number was about to change.

Don Cobra's copter bounced in next, dropping off the weary but successful JAWS team.

All that remained now was to recover the giant re-Americanized C-130 gunship and its escorts. According to the others in the recovery force, the big plane and its chickens were about twenty minutes behind the helicopters.

While waiting for them, the deck crew went back to stacking water bags.

Hunter needed sleep.

He'd spent most of the 48 hours leading up to the Matterhorn mission crawling around inside the giant gunship, lashed as it was to the deck, as it was too big to be brought to the hangar sections below.

He'd spent those two days studying every control, lever, pedal, wire and button, determined not to miss even the slightest detail as to why the beast flew the way it did.

At the end of it, he concluded the gunship was an overly complicated yet still terrifying remotely-controlled—or, once again, better put: self-controlled—aerial weapon the likes of which the world had never seen.

Simply speaking, the "Z-130" —they'd re-named it after the Zabiz Tribe—had been flown by an autopilot which in turn took its instructions from a pre-programmed radio message running in loops inside a radio transmitter. This device sent out radio signals to the plane's flight controls just like a pilot would if a human had been at the stick, taking its cues from the massive array of electric eyes in the plane's nose.

But this self-control extended beyond the plane's flight capabilities and into its weaponry and even tactics. This plane's instruments had been set to detect any kind of interference specifically with the Tangiers nuclear mine, which was continuously transmitting a signal back to the airplane essentially saying all was in working order. If that signal was altered in any way, (as in the shocks he and Cookie had endured) the air beast would come to life, take off and go after the interloper with its insanely-powerful array of weapons.

It'd happened twice at the Tangiers Dam with this plane and now again in Switzerland with a bright orange one. That there was more than one of them was now an acknowledged fact among the UA. These airplanes were built for one purpose, to live and die in the blind service of protecting a madman's mad dream.

But here's where it got really strange. While this plane had a very convoluted yet sophisticated collision avoidance system that kept it from slamming in the water, or the dam, or even Hunter's F-16XL during their brief dogfight, it didn't have any kind of targeting system for its overload of weaponry. It really was an alarmingly simple case of point everything in one direction, engage the triggers and hope for the best.

The big plane was never meant to be a precision weapons system. Again, all that firepower and flash and smoke, flames and screaming whistles—it was all meant to terrify. Like the dragon in a myth. The fear of it is almost as bad as the thing itself.

In any case, all of that Viktor-ish radio-controlled gear was gone now. With help from Ben and JT and some expertise from the SPOOC guys, Hunter had managed to get rid of all the automatic stuff and turn the plane's controls back into what they'd been designed for in the first place: to be flown by a human being.

So what kind of plane did they have now? It wasn't a bomber, although it could probably carry a substantial bombload under its wings. It was no longer a cargo plane because almost every square inch of its insides was taken up by something having to do with the weapons' array or ammo storage. That really only left one designation: What was once meant more to scare opponents to death than to perforate them, Hunter now had what had to be the biggest, baddest, fighter-bomber in the world.

While all of the Viktor-deigned gizmos had been removed, the vast arsenal the plane carried remained. The quartet of gigantic GAU guns sitting right beneath the flight deck had no place in any kind of aircraft, yet here they were. The mechanisms used to keep these fierce weapons continuously firing were brilliantly complex especially when first placed in the A-10 Thunderbolt. GAUs fired ammunition so powerful, a single round could destroy a tank. And each of the four guns onboard was loaded with hundreds of rounds. Correctly applied, this sort of firepower could cause apocalyptic mayhem on whatever it was shooting at below. Having these gigantic weapons do their thing just a few inches below his boot heels was almost surreal.

There was just one trigger for the fearsome foursome, fire one fire them all. There was one other trigger; it controlled all the guns sticking out of the big plane's huge wings and the turret up top.

Again, Hunter left all these weapons in place. But there was no way he could come up with a real targeting system for all that gear in the UA's continuously shrinking timetable. So, he was stuck with point and shoot.

JT had served as his co-pilot on the Matterhorn mission. Now, his friend took over the controls of the giant gunship just as they passed back out over the Med, flying low over the city of Genoa.

Like Hunter, JT was a seasoned fighter pilot with many hours in the air and in combat. Though a little woozy from the roller coaster ride he and Hunter had just gone through, resulting in a quick end to the Orange Alps Monster, he was eager to get behind the gunship's wheel and see what it was like flying one of Viktor's craziest weapons.

They rendezvoused with their high air cover escorts just a few miles off Genoa. These two Su-34s were flown by Ben Wa and Captain Crunch and their co-pilots and they'd watched the entire Matterhorn encounter while circling 10,000 feet above the famous peak.

During his two-day cramming session aboard the Z-130, Hunter had managed to install the necessary gear so the big plane could refuel in-flight. By design then, Ben and Crunch were flying Su-34 buddy tankers, in-flight refuelers that still retained their fighting and bombing capabilities.

Strictly for precautionary reasons, they knew it would be wise to top off the big plane's fuel tanks at this point. Should a complication arise during the gunship's unorthodox landing procedure, it would be good if they didn't have to worry about the gas while trying to figure out how to fix the problem.

JT handled the in-flight refueling session. It proved flawless, and once gassed up, the three planes turned south and headed back to the carrier in earnest.

It was a calm night, the half-moon was just starting to rise. They were all running on caffeine and bennies, a form of speed frequently given to pilots looking at long missions. Though Hunter had had a go around with bennies about a year before, he was able to handle them now simply because with all the coffee he drank, he barely noticed the buzz.

At least that's what he managed to tell himself.

They were soon just twenty miles out from the carrier; so close they could start to make out its landing lights on the dark horizon.

Suddenly, Hunter felt an uneasy vibration run through him. He immediately sat up straight and became mega-alert. He knew this feeling—and he didn't like it.

"Something's not right," he said to JT.

JT had seen his friend like this many times and he knew it was always wise to take it seriously. The Wingman was rarely incorrect about these things.

"Something's up with 'The Force?' " JT asked as Hunter first checked their radar and seeing nothing, went to each cockpit window, looking out into the night sky hoping to spot whatever was tripping his internal early warning system.

Then he saw it. Out the window to his right. A bright flare of light coming over the horizon about 50 miles to their northeast.

A missile . . .

He studied the speck of fire tearing across the sky, at the same time doing some high-speed calculations in his head. Velocity, height, trajectory—the numbers didn't lie. The missile was heading right for the USS *USA* . . .

Hunter and JT did three things in the next few seconds. JT radioed Ben and Crunch in the buddy tankers and quickly told them the situation. They in turn dropped their extra fuel tanks and became clean attack fighters again. At the same time, Hunter radioed the ship with the urgent news that they were about to be attacked.

Then the three UA planes started a long sweep to the northeast from where the missile had come. A few moments into this turn, they saw a large explosion light up the night off to their south about 15 miles away. It was the incoming missile being destroyed by the *USA*'s anti-aircraft weapons.

This was just what they wanted to see. The carrier's defensive systems had worked.

Now it was time to find out who took the shot at them.

Ben was the first to reach the spot where they'd believed the missile had been fired.

But nothing was there—nothing but miles of open water.

He swore softly on seeing this. They'd hoped to find an island out here with a missile base on it, perhaps owned by some Med pirates who felt entitled for some transit fees from the USS *USA* passing through.

But no island could only mean one other thing: some kind of fast attack boat.

And properly equipped with the right crew and weaponry, a fast attack boat could be dangerous even to a behemoth like the *USA*.

They searched all night.

Hunter and JT in the Z-plane, half the Su-34 squadrons from the carrier and the full 40-plane complement of the Flying Knights Yak-38 contingent.

All of the carrier's anti-sub copters were involved in the search too, as were its Mi-24 gunships and even the Slugboats.

But there really weren't a lot of places to hide.

They were in the farthest northern reaches of the Med, facing the northwestern part of Italy, off Genoa, Recco and Rapallo. These days this region was little more than a few hundred miles of rocky and exposed coastline with only a handful of working ports, all of them small.

The Americans formed a wide search pattern, broken up into grids with some Su-34s converting into electronic search planes and sending crude but live video maps to everyone else. At last doing what they were built for, the

Ka-27s dragged all of the port harbors with sonar equipment. And anywhere it seemed a boat could come to shore, a group of Flying Knights would land their VTOL jets and canvass the area on the ground. Somewhere in the middle were Hunter and JT, in the Z-plane, all loaded up with nowhere to go.

This was something the crew of the *USA* could do and do very well, conduct a wide combat search, involving hundreds of square miles in the middle of the night on extremely short notice. No other country in the world these days could perform such an operation, never mind just a single ship.

But in the end the search was fruitless.

Nothing was ever found.

The sun came up and after one last sweep came up empty-handed, the decision was made to bring all the aircraft back on board and move on.

Chapter Sixteen

Tuk the bodyguard had never been to this part of the Mediterranean before.

Growing up in what used to be Hungary, he'd never been more than a mile away from his village before Khan and his army arrived, ransacked the place, sparing his life only because he was big, strong and dumb, what every person wanted in a bodyguard.

That had been nearly two years ago, and in that time, Khan's Army had taken over most of the Balkans as well, receiving a substantial amount of their supplies to do so from ships operated by pirates. But most of that larder came in through a crappy war torn port in Croatia called Split. It was a dark, dirty and dangerous place with horribly polluted water and perpetually smoggy air. It looked like something from the Dark Ages and Tuk hated going there.

But now, here he was, still in the Med but in a place that to Tuk looked like paradise. The water was warm and clean, the skies were clear and sunny and the scenery was somewhere beyond breathtaking.

It was called La Macinaggio or La Mac for short. It was located on the northeast side of Corsica, the large island about 200 miles off Italy's west coast.

Corsica was once part of France and in the pre-Big War years, there was a secret submarine base at La Mac. Very active in the 1960s, it was here that French nuclear subs would get replenished in the middle of the night and then resume their hunt for their Russian counterparts deep beneath the Mediterranean.

All activity at La Mac ended with the Big War and the place was simply abandoned. Years later, it still featured not only picture postcard backgrounds, but many places where ships of all sizes could hide. From beneath low vines falling off its high cliffs, to actual concrete sea pens built into the side of the island's north face, concealing a giant nuclear submarine—or many, many smaller but no less dangerous vessels—was almost too easy to do.

The pirate gang that Khan's army dealt with most regularly was called the Red Flags.

They operated all over the Med, boasting a fleet of 22 Russian-built Osa fast attack boats, all with well-trained and veteran crews. When not preying on innocent shipping inside the Big Lake, they also served as carriers of illicit cargo—guns, drugs, girls. Frequently they made more money hauling stuff for Khan than they did at pirating.

Though not their typical MO, when Khan approached the leader of the Red Flags with an offer of $10 million in gold if they managed to sink the American's supercarrier—with as many anti-ships missiles they would ever need—there was no way the pirate leader could say no.

This was how Khan essentially bought himself a navy, basically betting $10 million that the Red Flags could actually sink the mighty *USA* using its new weapon of choice, the Silkworm missile.

The huge anti-ship rocket was a good fit for the Osa attack boats; one Osa could launch one or even two of the giant missiles at a target 80 miles away and then leave the area at high speed before anyone knew what had happened.

There were lots of advantages to sailing the largest warship ever built.

Just on size alone, most potential adversaries took one look and changed their minds. If you were with the good guys, there was not a sweeter sight than to see it come over the horizon. If you were a bad guy, that silhouette would make you start thinking of maybe going somewhere else, quickly.

On the downside, it was hard to keep the movements of a ship the size of the USS *USA* secret for very long inside the Mediterranean. Though nothing like the pre-Big War days, there were still communications networks in use around and on the sea. News moved quickly on them, especially when it was about something as imposing as the USS *USA*.

It was seen going through the Strait of Gibraltar two days before and was later spotted sailing by the island of Ibiza and then again off the coast of the long-dead gilded playground of Monte Carlo. By that time, word had gotten around that while it seemed to be paying particular attention to the area around Genoa, it also appeared the mighty warship was gradually sailing east. At that point Khan ordered the Red Flags to get every available Osa to La Mac asap. By nightfall that day, there were a dozen of the fast attack boats docked at the abandoned secret base and another ten were on their way.

Later that night, one Osa was sent out on a special mission. Its orders were to fire a lone missile at the American carrier after it was spotted about 50 miles off the coast of Genoa. But unbeknownst to the Osa's crew, their boat had been secretly wired with explosives. Once they fired the missile, it was blown to smithereens via remote control. Not only did this kill the entire crew, but it sent the boat's wreckage to one of the deepest parts of the Mediterranean, out of range of even the best underwater detection gear.

So when the Americans came looking for their attacker, there was nothing to be found, no clue to who shot at them or why.

The idea behind this suicide mission was to judge the level of American response to a small, pin-prick type attack. If they'd sent out a search plane or two, or wound up doing nothing at all after being fired upon, that would indicate that they were avoiding confrontation and this would make them an easier opponent than they might have thought.

As it turned out, the UA sent out dozens of planes and searched for hours. *That* was proof of their level of commitment—and that was a little worrisome.

The Widow told Khan and the others that she didn't think the best way to sink the American ship was in one massive attack. Instead she suggested they just batter it mercilessly with a lot of smaller hit-and-run actions. Kill it with a thousand cuts. Make its death slow and painful—and if and when it goes down, then you can pick up your 1,000 pounds of gold.

But there was a problem with this approach—and even someone like Tuk knew it. True, there were many adversaries around the world today that could be conquered or at least discouraged by a war of a thousand cuts. Just keep up with the pinpricks, be small but relentless, and drain them slowly of blood and treasure until they either sink or turn around and go home.

Not the Americans though. Khan and his men knew what had happened to Viktor's Siberian A-Bomb factory not that long ago. They also knew what happened in Hamburg and in Tokyo Bay.

The Americans weren't just powerful, they were unpredictable, even crazy. They razed nearly half of downtown Hamburg as a *distraction* for rescuing one of their spies that had been caught by the Russians. And they'd made Tokyo Harbor a sinkhole for hundreds of years to come—just to get a chance at offing their national bogey man, Viktor Robotov, for good.

You don't kill something like that by cutting it 1,000 times because you're not going to get past three or four before the people you wanted to make bleed turn around and come after you to do the same thing. And he didn't know why, if anybody, the Widow didn't understand this.

But then again, there was $200 million in gold at stake here—$190 million if the Red Flags came through. So maybe it made sense to at least give it a try.

To this end, La Mac was chosen not just for its secretive location but also on the thought that Khan's hired navy could continuously ambush the carrier as it resumed its journey through the Med, sailing down the west coast of Italy and squeezing its way past Corsica.

That's why Tuk was here.

With so much at stake, Khan wanted to be on hand when the carrier showed up—and where Khan went, so did Tuk.

They'd helicoptered to this place from a base in Bulgaria, a long bumpy uncomfortable journey that featured no less than five landings to gas up, all of them in very wild and wooly places along the way.

But now here they were, on the high cliff overlooking La Mac, watching the Osa boats zooming back and forth across the tiny bay below, each carrying two enormous Silkworm missiles, apparently ready for anything.

This was how the day passed. The Osa crews getting used to having the big anti-ship missiles on board and doing maneuvers further out to sea, perfecting their tactics for the upcoming ambush.

Night fell and as usual, Tuk laid out his bedroll just outside Khan's living pod, the best place to protect his boss. This positioned him just a few feet from the cliff's edge. From here, he could hear the movement of the sea below, and feel the cooling wind rushing by. The spectacular night time views made it all the better.

But then it happened again.

He'd just lay down and started counting the stars when a glint of light out over the bay caught his eye. It was like a red sparkling candle, flying fast but erratically. It only lasted a second or two but it was long enough to get his attention.

He sat up and tried to find it again in the murk. A minute went by with no luck, so he lay back down again and this time, closed his eyes.

Just a few seconds later, he heard a loud pop followed by a back-firing noise. He opened his eyes again and to his horror, just a few hundred feet from the top of the cliff, illuminated by fiery exhaust coming from its weird sounding engine, was a small plane with giant wheels and painted in bright, circus colors.

Something a clown would fly.

It was gone a second later, leaving Tuk to question his sanity, and not for the first time.

Was that thing real?

Or did he just imagine it . . .again?

The next day passed with an uneasy calm.

Tuk remained atop the cliff with his boss, again looking out over the water and watching the missile boats move back and forth within the sheltered harbor of the island. Some new arrivals were loading up with Silkworm missiles. Others were test firing their other deck weapons.

Tuk sensed a wave of bravado throughout the base. A buzz was going through the Red Flag pirates like a wildfire. Just attacking the American carrier alone would put their name on the lips of the dozens of marauding armies roaming the post-Big War landscape.

But how famous would they be if they actually sank it?

That's how it was these days, Tuk knew. It wasn't enough that you beat some other shit-bum army, you had to let everyone know about it.

But he did not share the excitement of the pirates; instead he was very anxious. He didn't tell anybody about what he saw the night before just like he never mentioned it to anyone the first time he thought he saw the strange little airplane. As a result he kept expecting something bad to happen. Khan stayed inside his personal module all day, planning his guerilla war at sea, a series of quick hit and run attacks against the big ship, just as the Widow had suggested. Tuk had no choice but to wait outside and count the minutes as the day crept by.

There were some distractions though. He watched with much interest, and a little easing of his concern, as Red Flag manned anti-aircraft sites began popping up all over the La Mac. Everything from Bofors dual-barrel

AA-guns to small Strelya Russian-built towed AA missiles and even a few Stinger batteries. Any air attack on La Mac would be a difficult proposition now with all this weaponry installed and pointing skyward.

Tuk knew some of the AA sites came with air raid warning sirens, just like in olden days. Not that they were needed—everyone here was familiar with the sound of AA fire going off. Missiles whooshing or big guns pom-poming away. Once you heard it, and witnessed its volume and intensity, it was hard to forget. With all these weapons, flying through the combined barrage would be hell for any pilot, including American ones. Or at least that's what Tuk tried to tell himself.

By sundown, Tuk became numb to his concerns and in this way, they faded away for the day. A bottle of vodka with his evening meal of powdered eggs also helped ease his mind. By the time he laid out his bedroll again, he was nearly whistling. Worrying was just praying for things you didn't want. And besides, maybe he'd gotten it wrong all along. Maybe the Americans would decide this fight was not for them and turn around and head for home. And maybe the Widow will pay them anyway.

By the time he laid his head down, he was laughing and whispering: "The Americans are cowards . . . All of them . . . Cowards . . ."

The air raid sirens went off a few seconds later.

Chapter Seventeen

Although what happened next would be recounted by many people many times over, most agree it all started with a single flare.

Once the sun went down, it became pitch black around the secret base, all lights either *verboten* or properly covered over. The sea around the area was also jet black, with no moon yet, barely any breeze and no waves anywhere.

So when the flare went off about a thousand feet above the bay that protected the secret base, it caught the attention of a lot of people on the ground. At first they thought it had been launched from one of the hidden attack boats by mistake.

Then with everyone who was awake looking at it as it slowly descended towards the harbor, something else went over the base and in its wake it left an entire string of parachute flares. Two dozen in just a couple seconds.

That's when all the base's anti-aircraft weapons opened up.

Which was exactly what the Americans wanted.

The first wave of Su-34 fighter bombers came in once the anti-aircraft barrage had reached its peak.

Now the sky was indeed as bright as day, which actually helped the American pilots find their targets. These were mostly radar-guided AA batteries shooting at them. The first wave of Su-34s carried HARM missiles, anti-radiation weapons that honed in on a target's radar signal. In this way, more than a dozen AA sites were picked off all in the mere seconds it took for this leading vanguard of UA jets to roar over the target.

With many of the AA sites now in flames, a second wave of the strike force arrived. Two dozen of the Yak-38 jumpjets flown by the Flying Knights came in super low, some below 100 feet, firing their cannons directly into the base, still illuminated by the slowly falling flares, the burning AA sites and the remaining AA fire itself.

The Yaks were armed with incendiary rounds. They strafed command buildings, a barracks and a fuel depot along the cliffs beside the bay. Many secondary explosions followed and within just a few more seconds, the fires around La Mac, already bright and intense, started to rage out of control.

Even before one minute had elapsed, more than half the base was already in flames.

Stunned and nearly frozen in place, Tuk and Khan watched in horror from the cliff as the attack on the base continued with sickening precision below.

Acting more out of panic than following orders, some of the missile boat captains were putting to sea, foolishly revealing their hidden positions.

Seeing this, Khan furiously tried to raise someone on the radio, but all of the base's communications seemed to be dead or dying. When one lone and confused voice finally answered him, Khan started screaming into the microphone that all attack boat captains should get back in their hiding places which at least would keep them away from the attacker's bombs.

But it was too late.

About half of the base's Osas were trying to get away from the burning base, trying to flee. That's when the Z-130 gunship made its first appearance.

It came out of the north, as had the rest of the UA raiders. It was flying low and its smoke screen was activated. What came next was the total air monster show. The flames, the smoke, the whistling death. It caught many of the missile boats out in the open. They were so clustered together in the panic of the moment, a two second burst from the Z plane's four GAU's was all it took to sink more than a dozen of the small warships.

Then just like that, it was gone. The flames, the smoke, the noise—the simple giganticness of it all—had disappeared into the night. More than half the Osa attack boats had been sunk or were in flames in the bay. And still the air raid was less than two minutes old.

That's when the third wave of American attack planes arrived.

In the next minute Tuk and Khan saw some astonishing things.

First, the big scary airplane made a long slow turn and was now firing at and sinking those last few missile boats who'd managed to get out of the secret harbor. Meanwhile on the peak across from them four Yak-28 jumpjets had landed and their pilots, now armed like Special Forces troopers, proceeded to seize the base radio station and radar dishes.

Then directly below them they saw four gray Mi-24 Hind helicopter gunships, flying very low and shooting at anything in the base that was not on fire or still moving.

And that's all it took. With less than three minutes elapsed in the battle, Khan's rented navy and his secret base were gone. Everything was either in flames or sunk or both.

But the biggest surprise was to come for Tuk and Khan.

Suddenly the wind was blowing fiercely behind them. They turned to see an Americanized Ka-27 naval helicopter bounce in for a landing. A half dozen soldiers in the cargo bay were pointing their weapons at them.

Tuk and Khan immediately raised their hands in surrender.

Four of the troopers leapt off the copter, ran forward and bound both Khan and Tuk's hands with zip ties. Khan was noticeably terrified during this procedure. Tuk was trying his best to control his emotions, but at the moment, failing miserably.

As they were being led back to the copter as prisoners, Khan couldn't take it anymore.

This perfect base, in the perfect location, had been utterly destroyed. Fires were raging everywhere. The docks were all on fire as were the command houses, the ammo dump and the base's fuel tanks. The bay was full of burning and sinking attack boats. The attack had lasted less than five minutes, yet the destruction had been absolutely complete, and almost overkill.

"Why?" Khan finally asked the American soldiers. "Why are you doing all this to us?"

One of them just shrugged and said: "This is what happens when you piss off the United States . . ."

Chapter Eighteen

It was the tallest building on the western side of the Bosporus Strait.

At 87 stories, 1,045 feet high, Mermesa Tower loomed over the European half of Istanbul, watching the ancient city like a big brother, seeing all.

Originally built as a five-star hotel, after the Big War it was taken over by the Saladin Gang, rulers of not just Istanbul, but of pretty much a new Ottoman Empire. They controlled the Bosporus, the very strategic waterway which essentially connected the Black Sea to the Med. Though nowhere near the amount of pre-Big War traffic used this passage, it was still very busy, mostly with drugs, arms or human trafficking shipments.

No one went through in either direction without paying a substantial fee to the Saladins. The bigger and badder your cargo, the more you had to pay. That was the price of doing business in this post-apocalyptic world. You got your stuff where it had to go and the Saladin Empire was able to further enrich itself and add even more war toys to its already large military.

The Tower now was a combination command headquarters, presidential palace and, on the top floor, an ultra-exclusive nightclub. It was done very much in the go-go style of the pre-Big War years, lots of secluded tables, subtle lighting and a long glass bar intended for both serving drinks and snorting cocaine.

It wasn't a case of you had to *know* somebody to get invited up here. Rather you had to *be* somebody, or you wouldn't get anywhere near the exclusive elevator that went straight up to the club. Those at the top of the Saladin Gang food chain could usually be found here at night along with their corps of bodyguards. Another small army of staff and servants attended to their every need—except one. This was why yet another small army, one consisting of high price call girls, was usually in attendance as well.

As the tallest building for miles around, the views from the nightclub were spectacular, especially at night. This was why the very top of the tower featured an array of large red blinking lights, of the same kind as used at airports, warning beacons to prevent airplanes from smashing into the skyscraper.

Though it was an almost enforced party atmosphere in the club one story below and the cocaine use sometimes reached blizzard proportions, the talk among the Saladin chiefs did not avoid world events. Their vast empire allowed them to have intelligence assets in many parts of Europe and Asia and their daily reports were always good fodder for conversation up in the tower.

At the moment the entire Med was abuzz with the unexpected appearance of the United Americans' gigantic aircraft carrier, the USS *USA*.

No one was sure why it was suddenly in their backyard. The previous year it was well known that the American carrier had spent a lot of time in the Pacific, fighting various bugaboos, real or imagined, an adventure that wound up very badly for Tokyo Harbor as it was nuked by those same Americans in their neverending effort to kill the super-villain, Viktor Robotov.

The ship was said to carry nearly one hundred war planes, by far the largest concentration of naval power in the post-Big War world. Plus, it seemed like the long standing rumor that the Americans secretly had nuclear weapons aboard had been confirmed, as the residents of Tokyo would attest.

And now, for some reason, they were here in the Med.

Borak Ozturk was a general in the Saladin Gang; his responsibilities included the protection of Istanbul and its surrounding areas. More like a police chief than a military officer, he knew everyone and everyone knew him.

One of his duties on nights like this was to procure a fresh collection of call girls to liven up the party. Ozturk imported girls from all over, but only the best of the best in his opinion made it up to the top floor of the Mermesa. He prided himself on getting the most sensual looking women money could find, but also paid close attention to what his bosses liked. Styles changed. Tastes change. Redheads, brunettes, even metallic-haired beauties come and go.

But two never, ever went out of fashion: blondes and raven-haired beauties.

So, for this night, he'd procured two of the most beautiful women he'd ever seen fitting those types. The blonde was almost regal, stunning features, soft blue eyes, killer smile—and everything else. She was wearing a little black dress with a plunging neckline, black stockings and smoking black heels. The raven-haired beauty was dressed in a long, tight, nearly transparent black gown with puffy sleeves and sexy buckle boots.

For some reason, she reminded Ozturk of a pirate.

They'd been seated at the head of the bar, places of honor in a way, because the big boss's table was just an arm's reach away.

And with these two beauties sitting so near, Ozturk knew they wouldn't be at the bar very long.

Mehmet Sadik was the vice supreme commander of the Saladin Gang, basically it's second in command. He'd noticed the two women at the end of the bar as soon as he reached the top floor night club.

It was almost midnight now and Sadik, a regular here, grabbed a drink and walked right over to them, his two bodyguards in tow.

Seeing all this, Ozturk was near triumphant; his big, big boss was going to get laid tonight, at least once. Maybe multiple times.

And Sadik would remember who provided him with this night of memories. He was that type of guy.

About thirty minutes and a few drinks later, Ozturk spotted Sadik heading up to the tower's roof with the two beauties.

Ikramiye! he whispered to himself. "Jackpot . . ."

As a building the Mermesa was grand in many ways, but it was the roof where everyone wanted to be—or at least visit.

Spectacular didn't come close to describing the view up here at night. The big city cut in half by a river and straddling two continents, glowing lights everywhere, even out on the water.

The Saladin Gang were by no means soft hearts. You didn't build an empire like theirs by being meek. But more than a few of them who'd seen this view commented that it almost looked the way it looked 1,500 years ago, when this place was Constantinople and it pretty much ruled a very large part of the civilized world.

There was no doubt the magnificence of this place wowed the ladies too. It was said it never failed to put them into romantic moods, even the high class hookers.

Another half hour went by. The club was really starting to rock with electro disco music blaring and lots of coked-out people trying to dance. But Ozturk became concerned. His boss had yet to return. He knew how long these things usually took—and even times two, Sadik should have reappeared by now.

Already drunk and buzzed himself, Ozturk got the strange urge to go upstairs and see if his boss needed a hand—at doing anything.

So, after one more shot of Papazkarasi and another massive bump, up he went, ascending the marble staircase to the stars, two steps at a time.

The first thing he noticed coming out of the access door was the wind—it was blowing crazily even atop a place where a steady 30 M.P.H. breeze was commonplace.

But this was definitely more than a breeze. This was more of a down draft. It was also very noisy up here . . . unusually so.

The roof was laid out like a modern version of a Caligula play room. Lots of marble statues doing sophomorically sexual things, stone elves urinating into fountains, that sort of thing. For the most part it was also dark up here, save for the continuous blinking of the six huge red aircraft warning lights. But even something about them was off, though Ozturk couldn't immediately figure out what.

Then he found Sadik. His big boss was propped up against a marble wall, naked except for the pair of underpants pulled up and over his head. His uniform was gone as were his side arms. He looked dead but was actually unconscious. Despite his rather awkward appearance, Ozturk could see the man was breathing heavily as his underwear was inflating and deflating in a rapid motion.

He also looked like someone had just kicked the crap out of him. And there was no sign of the two beauties he'd climbed up here with.

The crazy wind got Ozturk's attention again. That's when he looked up into the dark to see a helicopter directly overhead. It took a moment for him to put two and two together.

But then he finally realized the copter was taking off from the building, meaning it had landed here sometime before.

Dangling from under its fuselage was one of the large red beacons situated atop the roof to prevent airplanes from crashing into it. That's why their combined light was a little dimmer. One of them had been disconnected and was being carried away by this helicopter.

None of this made any sense to Ozturk, and it was about to get worse.

The helicopter quickly faded into the night to be replaced by something even more confusing. High overhead he saw what at first he believed was a large airplane on fire. That turned out not to be the case, but there was an airplane way up there that was covered with a cloud of smoke as it moved across the sky.

If that wasn't strange enough, he suddenly saw a second huge airplane with the same moving smokescreen suddenly appear. Incredibly the two planes started circling each other like fighters in a ring. But the third time around, the first big plane suddenly did what looked like an almost impossible bone crushing banking maneuver, firing a huge arsenal of weapons from its nose as it was doing so. To Ozturk, it looked like this plane had opened its mouth and a stream of pure fire came out of it.

Like a dragon, he thought.

The barrage of flame caught the second plane dead-on and it exploded in mid-flight. It was such a powerful blast that it resulted in millions of tiny pieces of debris which began to fall on Istanbul like a rainstorm of sparks.

Apparently completing what it was here for, the victorious air beast turned again and disappeared to the west.

At that moment, Ozturk actually wondered if he was too high. Because what he'd just seen was something more likely to show up in a dream, a bad one.

He shook some sense back into himself and finally rushed over to help Sadik.

But in all the screwiness of what he'd just witnessed in the last minute or so, one question stood out from the others: Why would anyone want to take one of the Mermesa's red warning lights?

Chapter Nineteen

The place was called Besiktas-Bogazi.

It was an enormous port facility in the Dardanelles region of Turkey, on the western side of the Bosporus Strait, about 150 miles south of Istanbul. A forest of enormous but deteriorating heavy-lift cranes, some of which soared 500 feet above the ground, there was a time before the Big War when "Bee-Bo" was one of the most important places in the world. On the border of Europe and Asia, sailing vessels from all over had been coming here for centuries. It was literally the place where east met west.

While Bee-Bo still held a reputation as a crossroad of sorts, any cargo that went through the place these days was most likely to be drugs, weapons or victims of human trafficking—or sometimes all three. The nearby population had mostly faded away after the Big War; some of those who remained behind turned the port into a bad version of a post-apocalyptic movie set. Murderous gangs roamed the place now, something akin to tribal warfare was common here, freaks fighting other freaks for everything and nothing.

In a very unpleasant world, this was one of the most unpleasant places.

The problem was, this was where Viktoria believed another hidden nuke could be found.

It had come to her one night, after she and Dominique had spent close to 24 hours trying to piece together what would come to be the fifth bomb's location. The long day ended in failure and one very tired hug because in this case, no matter which way they put the hundred or so drawing scraps together, the result never made sense. Their closest guess was a collection of very, *very* skinny elephants—on roller skates. Large creatures of some type with four legs and a trunk—but rail thin and on wheels? Giraffes on skateboards? In the middle of it all, something that looked like the tallest, skinniest minaret imaginable.

The various reconstructions of the drawing made no sense to Viktoria or Dominique or the guys on loan from SPOOC. The former pirate queen would have remembered going on safari in Africa and she didn't recall visiting any zoos during her trip with her father. No matter what they did, this time the puzzle pieces just refused to fall into place.

Once alone in her big cabin, Victoria tried to get herself into a trance as sometimes it helped her work through difficult issues. She did this by staring at her big purple candle and concentrating on the three separate flames. Clear the mind. Clear the soul. Let the memories flow back.

But she was almost too weary at this point to will herself into a spell, so her thoughts began to wander. How long had she owned this candle? It was enormous. Where did she get it in the first place? It might have been a gift, but where did it come from originally? Where was it made? Some candle factory somewhere, she supposed, but then how did it get into her hands? Certainly not by airplane or pack mule or . . .

She suddenly leapt from her bed and hurried back to the lighted table. She laid out the scraps of paper again, just as they had earlier that day, but now with a different thought in mind. Anything that moved around this planet pre- or post-Big War at some point was carried by a boat and at some point that boat went through a port.

And that's when it came to her. During the trip with her father, they'd visited this huge port facility and she remembered him taking hundreds of photos of it. It had been a dreary rainy day and she recalled two things: being wet and being in awe of the enormous cranes.

She immediately called Dominique, who reappeared at her door in five minutes with a pot of hot tea. Viktoria explained what she believed the drawing showed, and once tipped, Dominique could see the skinny elephants might be a bunch of very tall cargo cranes, the trunk being the lifting part of the crane itself, supported by the four long legs with wheels on the bottom to move up and down the pier.

But where was this port they'd visited?

Viktoria told Dominique she also remembered being very bored that day and that she'd complained to her father many times about how she wanted to leave.

Dominique thought a long moment. Cranky kid. Rainy day. KGB spy/father trying to keep it cool.

"Did he promise you something if you kept quiet?" she asked Viktoria. "A bribe perhaps to behave?"

Viktoria put her head in her hands and physically strained to remember. The pressure on her was reaching a breaking point. An examination of the Matterhorn device confirmed for them something they really didn't want to know: the moment they'd disconnected the Tangiers bomb, the Matterhorn bomb's timer was sped up by another 72 hours.

This meant in less than four days, any bombs they had not recovered would go off at exactly noontime GMT. And they were certain now that with each device they recovered and disconnected, that sped up all of the remaining timers, guaranteeing an even further shrinking deadline.

All this and more felt like the weight of the world on Viktoria's pretty shoulders.

Being a hero?

Saving the world?

It sure wasn't for everybody.

But then suddenly, her eyes brightened and she began to smile. It was like a locked room had been suddenly opened.

"To shut me up," she began slowly, trying to remember every detail, "he took me to what he called the most famous restaurant in the world and said I could get anything I wanted. But the only reason I wanted to go was because it sounded like he was saying: 'Mermaid,' and that's what I always wanted to be. A mermaid. I still do . . ."

"Was it The Mermesa?" Dominique asked her urgently.

Viktoria's eyes went wide again. "Is that a real place?"

"It's a very famous place in Istanbul," Dominique told her. "Lots of spies and shady people gather there now, along with the higher echelons of the Saladin Gang, the people who run the show in Turkey. But before the war it probably *was* the most famous restaurant in the world. Or one of them, at least."

Viktoria couldn't believe it. But the best was yet to come.

Out of the blue, Secure 9's phone rang once. It was the guys in the SPOOC. They'd been working on another drawing, the one they called Pile 5.

They asked Viktoria if she remembered going to Turkey during the trip with her father, because with a little imagination, Pile 5 could be pieced into a pretty accurate representation of the Istanbul skyline, minarets among skyscrapers, spotlights in the night sky.

Viktoria looked at the phone and started laughing.

Then she said: "We'll call you back . . ." and hung up.

She was still laughing, now with pure joy.

"Istanbul is one of the spots," she told Dominique. "And I remember I got an enormous dessert but I was still so mad there weren't any mermaids."

Dominique was also excited but she was already thinking ahead.

"If he was trying to bribe you with dinner," she said, looking back at the drawing of elephants on roller skates, "then you must have been in a large port facility earlier that day not far from Istanbul."

They got out a map and close together, leaning over the planning table side by side, they excitedly scoured it for a large port facility.

It took only a minute when Dominique's finger landed on a place in the Dardanelles just south of the infamous battle ground of Gallipoli.

"Could it be called Besiktas-Bogazi?" Dominique asked her.

Viktoria's eyes lit up once more. She really was very beautiful when she was smiling.

"Oh my God," she said. "The Bee-Bo . . . That's it! I remember that funny name!"

They dissolved into another hug, which lasted for a long time.

Twenty-four hours later, Dominique and Viktoria were on their way to Istanbul.

And the Slugboats and the JAWs team were on their way to the Bee-Bo.

Chapter Twenty

At about the same time Dominique and Viktoria had been served their first drink on the top floor of the Mermesa, 135 miles to the southwest, the American recovery team was approaching the port of Besiktas-Bogazi.

It was the same six Slugboats as at Gibraltar, all of them armed to the teeth, each carrying a squad of JAWS troopers, also armed to the teeth. Both crewmen and troopers were dressed all in black with blackened faces where needed.

Cook was on the first tugboat; as always he was in possession of the Boop. Everyone around him had been involved in countless operations like this. But many of them would later say that going into Besiktas-Bogazi gave them an extra super case of the creeps. It was all those rusted monsters looking over everything, the wind blowing through them, making weird noises, at night, with a moon casting shadows everywhere. In the middle was a very tall white tower that Cook thought might have been an antenna of sorts, or maybe an enormous crucifix, though all things considered, this would be a strange place to put it.

Creepy . . . and this was before they even got to the place.

Once they'd arrived there was no shortage of places to dock. The facility stretched for nearly a mile along the west coast of the Bosporus. It was basically one long pier, and at the moment, it was totally empty, with not another vessel in sight. They could land just about anywhere.

Trying to give the team any edge she could, Viktoria had told Cook that she felt the nuclear mine was somewhere "close to the water." This was important because in the pre-operation briefing, when they all learned of the cluster of cranes at this place, they wondered if the bomb was going to be planted up high somewhere, as all of them had been so far. Gibraltar, Tangiers Dam, the Matterhorn. And soon, a tower in Istanbul, where the fourth nuclear mine was disguised as an aircraft warning beacon. Did this mean the Bee-Bo bomb was up on one of the soaring cranes—and the JAWS guys would have to climb 500 feet to find it?

No, Viktoria had told them. She wasn't getting that vibe. "Near the water" is what she said.

The six Slugboats tied up along a main access dock just about in the middle of the huge port. It was very dark down here and the shallow but fast moving water of the Bosporus looked ominous and black.

Just like at Gibraltar, each Slugboat was carrying two quad-fifty mounts and some kind of antiaircraft weapon whether it be a Bofors AA gun or a Stinger missile. There was no need for any JAWS guys to stay behind and help guard the bulked-up tugs. The crews could do it themselves.

The full contingent of JAWS troopers quickly assembled on the dock and then went up the gangway to the port facility itself. If the place appeared creepy on their approach, it looked absolutely disturbing to them now.

The forest of high cranes rising out of the darkness was intimidating itself. But it was now apparent that many were not just in disrepair but actually falling apart. In fact they could see the remains of one that had already crashed to the ground, who knows when. It was lying in a long line of twisted steel wreckage like some kind of modern-day Colossus of Rhodes, stretching out of the facility and into the Bosporus itself.

They could also see fires burning up near the north end of the place, near the very tall white tower that might or might not be an antenna or a crucifix. The fires they were sure belonged to some of the wild gangs said to inhabit this place. They could also hear scattered gunfire and people screaming, but those sounds were well north of their position and sounded like they were coming from an old PA system.

There was an outer service road which ran the length of the port. On one side was a 20-foot corrugated wall topped with barbed wire. To get in amongst the cranes themselves, the team used *plastique* to blow a large hole in this barrier. It was a low-volume explosion. Once the smoke had blown away, the team checked their weapons and prepared to enter the huge facility.

During the two-hour voyage to this place, Cook and his men discussed what the weapon's disguise might be this time. Maybe another hydrant, or phone booth—or a chicken coop. They'd even considered taking bets on what they'd find next.

They'd only been half joking. But then, Cook went through the hole in the corrugated wall and saw what awaited them on the other side.

His heart sank.

"What *haven't* we found yet?" he groaned.

"An oil drum." someone replied, also in a groan.

Stretching out in front of them, from here to the far reaches of the facility itself, were tens of thousands of oil drums.

With the entire recovery team inside the wall a minute later, they all saw the task that lay before them. Go out into this jungle of greasy, slippery, extremely smelly oil drums, following the Boop, looking to see if the Holy Grail was among them.

This was *so* Viktor, they thought. Hiding the 3.5 kiloton IEDs in everyday items was one form of madness. But now it was like he was taunting them all the way from Hell itself. You may have had good luck finding everyday items in strange places. Now try to find one among many thousands—with a clock that's ticking down now even faster.

The team moved into the field of oil drums, walking slowly, in double lines, using their NightVision goggles to show the way. The glow of the tribal fires and the sounds of gunfire grew more apparent as they slowly made their way north. Meanwhile Cook was frantically moving back and forth in front of the two lines, sweeping the Boop over the barrels hoping to hear that magic buzzing sound indicating their prize had been found.

But that wasn't happening. Twenty minutes into the search, the device hadn't so much as burped.

By this time they were halfway across the dark and eerie landscape. The fires up ahead were glowing brighter, and the gunfire was louder as well. Then, soon enough, voices were being caught by their night goggles' super-ear sound detectors.

The column stopped, hunkered down and just listened. It took less than a minute of eavesdropping to determine they'd stumbled upon a very depraved group of individuals. There were about 200 of them, a quarter mile to their north, gathered in front of a dilapidated crane close to the 500-foot crucifix-ish white tower. Many of them were dressed in rags or less, dancing around an enormous bonfire. They were shouting and singing and continuously referred to themselves as the "Yam-Yams" in a kind of pseudo-English most of which the Americans could understand. But no one at the front of the JAWS column knew what Yam-Yams meant.

Next to the bonfire was a large roped off area looking like a very large boxing ring. The dancing and singing and the bonfire were all about a sort of fight club these people were engaged in. From the bits and pieces the Americans could pick up, they were apparently fighting each other to the death to see which one was going to lead a raid on a nearby village that next day.

It was clear that the unlucky village had no defenders, no food or weapons. Just lots of elderly unarmed people.

There were six potential commanders in the ring next to the bonfire at the moment. The rules were gruesomely simple: they would fight each other with knives, one on one, until only one was left standing. Whoever it was that would lead the attack the following morning.

The super-ears function on the UA's NightVision goggles worked surprisingly well. By zooming in on two or three individuals and listening in on their conversations, the Americans got a good idea what was going on, except one thing: They couldn't decipher why these people were raiding this defenseless village in the first place.

That's when word came up from the back that one of the Slugboat crewmen understood Turkish.

"That's impressive," Miller told Cook on hearing the news.

"Yeah—who knew?" Cook responded dryly.

The crewman was hustled up to the front, He found Cook, Miller, and about a dozen JAWS troopers concealing themselves behind the rows of barrels as the weird barbaric dance continued around the bonfire just 200 feet away.

Cook only had one question for him: "Any idea what Yam-Yams means in Turkish?"

The sailor looked back at him and almost laughed.

But then he saw Cook was deadly serious.

"I'm no expert, sir," the man told him. "But I think Yam-Yams means 'cannibals.'"

War of Dragons

On June 14, 1982, a fire destroyed three cargo ships docked at Bee-Bo, killing 12 people and burning down about a quarter of the facility.

The problem wasn't lack of water to fight the fires; it was the lack of pressure to pump water from the Bosporus to douse the flames. In order for Bee-Bo to reassume its rank as one of the most important ports in the world, the International Maritime Organization insisted they install new pumps but also construct a water tower as a back-up in case the new pumps failed.

That water tower was built the following year and when it was done, at 453 feet high, it qualified as the second tallest water tower in the world; only the 469-foot water tower in Mechelen, Belgium was taller.

Bee-Bo's tower was long and slender with a bulge about two thirds of the way up. In some ways, it looked like a flying saucer had somehow become stuck inside it. Other angles gave it a definite crucifix look. But at the same time, it looked like an odd minaret. Maybe the design's idea was to include all three. It was painted all white, just like the cranes at Bee-Bo, and was just about the same height. The water tower actually blended into the background of the gigantic facility.

As it turned out, JAWS CO Clancy Miller was looking at it right now. It was about 150 feet behind the bonfire where the Yam-Yams were still in the middle of their blood sport to see who was going to lead the apparently flesh-eating raiding party in the morning.

Miller grabbed Cook's shoulder and harshly whispered to him: "I hate to say this, but we've got to think like Viktor if we're going to figure this out."

Cook replied: "I'm listening . . ."

Miller waved his hand to indicate the vastness of the Bee-Bo port facility.

"A million oil drums, right?" he asked. "And the sort of guy Viktor is—or was—yes, on first thought he'd hide the nuke somewhere in here, needle in a haystack, right?"

"Right . . ." Cook agreed.

"And if the game played out the way he wanted it to, then he probably would have figured if we wound up here looking for the damn thing, then we're on to him as far as hiding it in everyday items . . ."

Cook nodded anxiously. "Please, go on . . ."

"But think about it," Miller continued. "The kind of guy he *really* was, he would have loved us to check every fucking oil drum in this place and not find anything. Why? Because we were looking in the wrong place all the time and with the clock ticking down every second."

Cook's usually super-calm demeanor was close to being tested.

"I'm open to suggestions, Clance," he told his old friend.

That's when Clancy pointed out the extremely tall water tower.

"He's into great heights for this joke," he said. "And that thing is actually the tallest thing here . . ."

"And all the barrels are just a distraction?" Cook said, mostly to himself.

Clancy nodded heartily. "And, like the lady said, she felt it was 'close to the water.' Well, it *is* a water tower . . ."

Cook turned his NightVision skyward and engaged a special zoom in function. It was like trying to spot something atop a 50-story building. But, damn, was that an oil barrel way up there?

They pulled back and rejoined the rest of the team about fifty feet behind them.

With all the squads gathered around, Cook gave a very quick briefing. He explained the situation to those who'd yet to see the dancing cannibals or the bonfire. He laid out the options of which there were few.

"There's forty of us," Cook told them. "And there's about two hundred of these mooks and they're armed."

"Maybe with forks and knives," Miller added.

"We don't want to lose anybody to those mushheads," Cook went on.

He studied the water tower and the surrounding giant skinny elephants and then the Bosporus beyond. Then he looked over at Miller. He was the team's explosive expert.

"So," he asked his XO. "What are the chances that if we blow that tower, everything including that can on top winds up in the river?"

Clancy thought a moment and then replied: "What are the chances the nuke goes off if we blow the tower?"

Cook just gave him a quick pat on the back.

"Exactly," he said. "Let's get the fireworks . . ."

Thirty more precious minutes ticked away.

The Yam-Yams were now down to the final two fighters in the ring. Both were torn and bloody from each killing two other men. With only these two left standing, the noise over the PA system became disturbingly loud and annoying. The music was atrocious and the majority of those in attendance were still caught up in the frenzied dancing.

This gave the JAWS guys the cover they needed to withdraw back to the service road, get some plastic explosives together and assemble a sapper team to deal with the gigantic water tower.

The only question was how much explosive to use. True, the tower was nearly 500 feet high, but it was less than ten feet wide and in theory it was either hollow inside or filled with water.

But it probably had a nuclear weapon on top.

"Ten pounds should do it,' Miller decided.

Though he didn't know why he said it, Cook replied: "Use twenty. Make sure it really goes down."

Miller gave him a mock salute. Then Cook handed him the Boop.

"Make sure first, though?" he asked his XO.

This time, Miller gave him a serious salute. Then he and two other explosives guys picked up their satchel bags and disappeared back into the night.

Cook, five of his troopers and the Slugboat crewman who understood Turkish returned to the oil barrel field, leaving the rest of the team to keep the service road and their escape route secure. Cook and his guys stole right back to their previous position. The Yam-Yams had worked themselves into a fever by now as the two last contenders for Commander of the Day were still relentlessly stabbing each other, knowing only one would survive.

The ring was covered with blood, as were lots of those who were standing up close to it. They seemed to relish it when a splatter of blood would hit them. The music never changed, but the dancing fools had become even more unhinged. The Americans could see some of them were now stabbing each other even as they were dancing; others were stabbing themselves. It was like something from a Borsch painting, a nightmare happening right before their eyes.

The minutes went by agonizingly slow. Finally Cook's radio buzzed.

It was Miller. "Charges are set," he reported. "It will drop right into the river. And your hula-hoop is still glowing. So, it's up there somewhere."

For the first time all night, Cook felt a tinge of relief. One way or another they had taken control of what they considered Viktor's fifth mine.

But now came the hard part. Cook was the commander on the ground, so it was his decision to make.

Blow the tower and just hope the device lands in a manner favorable to them when it hit in the water—and doesn't detonate.

Cook was a veteran warrior and he knew enough to ask himself, not just should he do it, but what would happen if he didn't. Get in a four-against-one firefight with some of the most depraved people on earth and then after somehow defeating them, climb a 500 foot tower, when every second was precious?

In the end it wasn't the hardest decision he ever made.

"Light it and give yourself a running start," he told Miller. "We'll meet you back at the road."

The charges went off four minutes later.

Miller and his team had stacked them on the east side of the gargantuan tower. In theory, the explosion should make the tower fall that way.

That's what they hoped.

Just before the explosives went off, they heard a mighty scream from the Yam-Yams camp. They could only guess that someone had finally won in the bloody ring. The music got louder, the PA system was all feedback now and the crowd of freaks were screaming madly, making the most disturbing sound of all.

Then the explosives went off.

The noise was tremendous, way more than Cook ever expected it to be. Somehow though the tower stayed upright—but only for a few seconds. And then it collapsed, the top of the tower landing about fifty feet out into the shallow water of the Bosporus, arriving with a great splash. It created a mini tsunami that the Slugboats had to ride out, but, a moment later that became the least of their problems.

Because as soon as the tower hit the water, they all heard an even louder sound, a roar and booming at the same time and they could see additional agitation under and atop the water where the tower had just gone in.

For a moment Cook was certain the nuclear device was about to detonate and this was what it was like when an A-bomb went off under water.

But then something else happened. He heard a voice calling him in his headphones.

It was Hunter.

He said just six words: "Get back to the boats, now . . ."

Then he was gone.

That was enough for Cook. No nuke went off and now Hawk was telling them to withdraw. That was definitely good by him. He smacked the oily ground in front of him twice with his gloved hand. No words need be spoken. As one, the team got up and double-timed it back to the Slugboats.

Tony 3 was not a big fan of flying.

And he was definitely not a big fan of flying while people were shooting at him even though he was shooting back.

But that's what he'd been doing for the past few hours, being violently tossed all over the sky, tracer rounds coming so close to him, he could see the sparks and sizzle as they went whipping by the canopy glass.

How does anybody do this? He swore if he made it to the ground alive, he'd never get in another airplane again.

But at the moment he was stuck here, strapped into the right-hand seat of the Z-130 gunship, holding on for dear life. That the person actually flying the plane was Hawk Hunter, the Wingman, and probably the best pilot ever, was of some comfort at the moment, but truly not much.

He'd had a front row seat for the battle above Istanbul against the air beast, that one had been painted all-black, and now they were racing towards the Dardanelles, to a place called Besiktas-Bogazi, where they were sure to meet yet another winged monster.

Tony 3 had already cried out a few times in the middle of some authentically scary flying, "Whose idea was this?' " only to be reminded by Hunter that it was Tony himself who put the current plan in motion.

They weren't up here to shoot down the air monsters, not really.

Actually they were trying to capture one.

Another one.

While Tony was the USS *USA*'s combat video guy, he was also an expert in all things radio. It was he who figured out at the last minute how to defeat a swarm of radio-controlled suicide drones sent by Viktor's South Pacific minions Yellow Star, to sink the mighty American aircraft carrier. So it was natural that he was intrigued by the air monsters and how they were radio controlled to the point of almost artificial intelligence. The things they could do was truly amazing, but as Tony knew better than everyone else, it was still radio—and that meant whatever was happening inside the air beast's auto pilot system could be jammed and possibly manipulated to do someone else's bidding.

Or at least that was the idea.

His idea . . .

It didn't work over Istanbul.

The air beast protecting the Istanbul device showed up right on cue. The moment Dominique and Viktoria hooked up the Ka-27's winch to the top of the red blinking light and were zapped by the electrical shock — they took it together—the beast was awakened. Hunter sensed it at that precise moment and told Tony it was coming. Using gear he'd lugged aboard the Z-130 and set up in the already crowded cockpit, Tony tried jamming the air beast's flight controls even before it showed up over the Mermesa Tower.

It did seem to have some effect on the big plane at first as the subsequent gyration high in the sky later proved. But for whatever reason, the beast's autopilot never fully clocked on to Tony's new frequency, so

Hunter had no choice but to shoot it down. Neatly carving it in two after the strange but brief aerial fight between the two flying leviathans, they watched it crash into the Black Sea.

Now they might have another chance over this place called Besiktas-Bogazi.

Even from 10,000 feet the place that was called Bee-Bo looked as advertised:

A long, wide strip of port facilities bordering the Bosporus Strait, highlighted by dozens of massive cranes that from this height looked like something from a sci-fi movie, mechanical giants, walking battleships or very large, very skinny elephants. They all looked frozen and rusting away and surrounded by many hundreds of sea-going cargo containers and what looked like thousands of oil drums.

In the middle of it all, Hunter and Tony could see a circle of people around a large bonfire.

When the huge water tower was blown up and toppled to the river, Tony 3 heard the Wingman say, "I guess it was up high after all." Then, not a half minute after Hunter radioed his warning down to Cook and the team to evacuate the port, Tony could see the distinct outline of an air beast coming right at them, same altitude, same heading.

"He's about five miles out," Hunter told Tony.

Tony immediately started twisting knobs, pushing buttons, flipping switches. In front of him was a long line of tiny light bulbs, going left to right in a rapid search for the frequency the airplane's flight controls were on and a frequency he might use to override it.

"OK—three miles," Hunter said just a few seconds later. Both planes were heading at each other at a closing speed more than 500 M.P.H. An airborne collision was just a few seconds away.

If it was a game of aerial chicken between the greatest pilot ever and a radio-controlled flight computer, then history would show that the unmanned plane blinked first.

Because just as Hunter was about to swerve off to his left, the air beast went right and began a shallow dive.

It was so extreme it could only mean one thing.

Hunter was quickly back on the radio with Cook.

"Our friends around the campfire down there," he said. "Are they boy scouts?"

Cook's reply was simple and quick: "Nope . . ."

In the end it didn't make any difference. The air beast dropped down to just 500 feet, took aim at the gathering of Yam-Yams warriors and opened up with its four gigantic Gatling guns, its eight wing mounted cannons and its quad-fifty top side turret.

Just like at the Tangiers Dam, it took only a few seconds to pulverize everything and everybody, cutting a swath through the port facility the size and length of three football fields.

One moment the Yam-Yams were there, the next, they were on the highway to Hell.

Hunter and Tony 3 had a God's eye view of what happened. Hunter knew if Cook deemed these guys to be bad guys, then there was no doubt the world would be better off without them.

But what did it say about the human condition that so many souls could be turned into microscopic dust in the blink of an eye? And have it done by a robotic, unthinking drone?

"It sucks to be them," Tony said, looking down at the carnage.

Hunter couldn't disagree.

A moment later his ESP kicked in again. The air beast was turning into a left hand climb as if to meet them head-on again.

"Juice up," Hunter said to Tony. "Let's try this one more time . . ."

It was almost a repeat of their first encounter. Both planes, at the same altitude, heading straight for each other at more than 500 M.P.H.

Tony ramped up his gear and started his scanner again. He'd told Hunter previously that the best way to do this was head-on. But in reality it was more of an educated guess than anything else.

But here they were.

Stomach flipping, the plane speeding towards oblivion, the flames and smoke still rising from the automated slaughter below, Tony fine-tuned his tuner—and suddenly the scanner stopped and stayed on one of its 13 red bulbs.

"Jessuzz, I'm in," Tony exclaimed.

He looked up and saw the oncoming plane quickly filling up the view on the cockpit windows.

"Now or never," Hunter reminded him as he stayed true to the collision course.

Tony punched in four buttons then turned his frequency switch all the way to the right. This, so he hoped, would insert a new flight command into the air beast's radio receiver, by-passing its original one. The first order given: Turn away.

Both men held their breath as nothing happened—for about two seconds. Then suddenly the air beast veered off and started a slow descent back in the direction of Istanbul.

Tony couldn't believe it. He was still shaking, but now in a good way.

"It worked," he said, incredulous of his own success. "It actually worked . . ."

They quickly turned and were soon on the tail of the air beast. They'd scoped out an airport early, mostly likely what was once Istanbul International. The place had been long since abandoned, but its runways were still there and though cracked and pot-holed, they were still serviceable, especially for an airplane with no one aboard.

But now came the hard part . . .

Tony started feeding the air beast some basic flight instructions, taking his cues from what Hunter was telling him.

"Down a little," Hunter was saying, essentially flying both planes at once. "Nose up, nose up . . . OK, now back to level."

Somehow it all worked. The big plane fell out of the sky and landed, wheels down, on the old cracked and cratered runway. It kicked up a lot of dirt and dust and its engines were overworked and smoking heavily. But it was more or less, intact.

Hunter and Tony did a fist-bump.

"And now we have two," Hunter said.

Chapter Twenty-One

The USS *USA* passed the island of Crete about an hour later.

At 00:30 hours, thirty minutes after midnight, the radio room received two encouraging messages: the JAWS guys had recovered the Bee-Bo nuclear mine from the Bosporus. Its protective cover was damaged from falling into the river, but as far as they could tell, the nuke was now stable and disarmed.

Second, another squad of JAWS guys had landed at the old Istanbul Airport, and along with Captain Crunch, were preparing to fly the captured, bright green gunship back to the carrier for, at the very least, a weapons harvesting.

Bull Dozer was up in the carrier's flight ops room in the ship's superstructure when the two messages came in. He was drinking a massive cup of coffee.

"In the old days I would've added some whiskey to this by now," he thought out loud, re-filling his cup. "I miss the old days . . ."

Dominique and Viktoria's recovery team had arrived an hour before, bearing the warning light beacon containing the fourth nuke mine. The SPOOC guys immediately examined the device and confirmed its time to detonation had been sped up as well. They were expecting the same from the Bee-Bo bomb.

In any case, the deadline had shrunk to less than two days. And they still had one bomb to go.

"Are we going to make it?" Dozer wondered. "Or will something trip us up?"

That pang of doubt became a brick of reality a moment later when his radio lit up. It was the Combat Control Center, two levels below.

"We have something unfriendly in-coming, sir," the stark voice on the other end said. It was the phrase no ship captain ever wants to hear.

"From where and what is it?" Dozer asked urgently.

"They're Silkworms again," was the reply. "Tracking in from the northeast. At least five blips. Arrival in about a minute."

Back when the UA destroyed Khan's hidden base on Corsica, those aboard the carrier wondered if that would be the end of the anti-ship attacks.

Now they needn't wait any longer for their answer.

"Enact defensive measures," Dozer yelled into the main comm. "Crew to battle stations . . ."

Then he drained his cup of coffee and started out for the War Room.

"Here we go again," he thought grimly.

*****

Hawk Hunter had experienced very few convergences of events in his life like the one he would have in the next ten minutes.

Almost a replay of them returning from the Matterhorn mission, as Hunter was approaching the USS *USA* in the Z-130 gunship; he got a message directly from Dozer telling him the carrier was under attack from Silkworm missiles—again.

And this time, it was more than one.

Hunter and Tony 3 were 20 minutes out from the carrier at this point. Close behind was Crunch flying the second air beast and behind them, the helicopter troop ships that had flown into Istanbul.

And about an hour behind everybody else were the Slugboats returning to the ship at full speed with the Dardanelles nuke mine under their control.

But now the carrier was under attack again.

Hunter's mind went in a hundred different directions at once. It was still night time—at least four hours before dawn. The seas were kicking up and another storm front was approaching. They would soon have to land two enormous planes, along with a bunch of helicopters, on the deck of the USS *USA*, in these conditions, with enemy missiles on the way.

"How many incoming?" Hunter asked Dozer.

"Six are now on the scope," he replied, adding ominously. "Make that seven . . . no eight. First is about thirty seconds from impact. We're geared up. Waiting for them to get in range. But we'll have to go eight for eight, and you know how hard it is to get a perfect score."

The carrier had some impressive close-in defensive capabilities. An array of anti-aircraft missiles lined both sides of the flight deck. There were also four CIWS modules (as in Close In Weapons Systems)—naval adaptions of the very same Gatling gun—which were able to put thousands of rounds directly in the path of any oncoming threat.

There were also several ManPad teams on the flight deck. Individual troops armed with shoulder launched Stinger missiles. A large contingent of this force was made up of the Zabiz Tribe soldiers, hearkening back to the original Missileers. Plus, there were all those bags of seawater piled up and down the deck.

Hunter ran the scenario through his head with a little glimpse into the future. His senses were telling him the ship could ward off the attack. But that still left too many questions. What if this was just a first barrage? Where were the Silkworms being fired from? And who had access to so many of the blunderbuss type anti-ship missiles in the first place? This was the second time the carrier was facing them in less than two days. No one on the carrier could ever remember being involved in any kind of combat situation where Silkworms had been used.

They'd all heard about them, but never saw one in action—until now when no less than eight were incoming.

Hunter leaned over to Tony 3 and just said: "Hang on..."

Tony knew it was coming, so he was physically prepared. But the mental acceptance was still a couple heartbeats behind.

"We're diverging from our course?" he asked as politely as possible.

"We're up here," Hunter answered putting the big gunship into a violent 5-g turn. "And we've got to find out where those Silkworms are coming from."

Tony understood, but that didn't mean he liked it. He was instantly pressed against his seat, barely able to breath for the g-forces.

"Whose idea was this again?" he gasped one more time.

The closest island now to the *USA*'s location was called Thira.

Located about 35 miles north of the carrier's current position, the island was about six miles long by two miles wide, with a low-slung, rocky mountain range serving as its spine.

Hunter had the island in sight within five minutes. Even from 20 miles out, they could see it was a chaotic scene.

At the moment the southern side of the island was lit up with raging fire and smoke. From the jungles below to the side of the narrow mountain range, bright orange launch trails from even more Silkworms taking off were plainly evident. So many of the missiles had been launched from here, there was a fiery yellow haze of exhaust encircling the entire island.

Hunter knew they had to attack this place now. He radioed back to Crunch who had his hands full at the moment. He was still learning how to fly his Z-130—and until now had been concentrating on how best to keep it in the air and then land it on the carrier. Now he had to figure out how to use its massive weaponry against their unseen but apparently well-equipped enemy.

"I think I can get the four big guns working," Crunch radioed back to Hunter. "Still trying to figure out the wing guns."

"Either way," Hunter told him. "Just point and shoot … and don't forget to engage your masking to avoid the AA fire. If there is any . . ."

By this time the island of Thira looked like it had been engulfed by a fireworks display gone wrong. That's how many Silkworms were being fired from the place. One was being launched every five seconds or so and the onslaught was relentless.

Typically any action involving big anti-ship missiles like the 'Worm meant two or three missiles at a time, tops. In fact, one usually did the trick on something smaller than the carrier.

That the people on this little island were throwing *dozens* of missiles at the *USA* in such a shot gun fashion was very odd.

The Americans could only hope that the carrier could avoid them all.

Crunch went in first.

He'd searched his control panel until he found the switch activating the plane's internally generated masking smokescreen, the one that made the Z-130 look like a fire-breathing dragon.

Two seconds after he flipped the switch, the entire plane was surrounded by a cloud of smoke following right along with them. He was amazed by the bizarre option the aircraft carried. But instead of being part of some psychological tactic or AA camouflage, to him it seemed like the whole plane was on fire.

He sighted up the middle of the island, an area where lots of missile trails were evident and, just like Hunter said, it was all point and shoot. He pushed the trigger and the kick from the four huge Gatling guns going off was so violent it seemed to hold the plane in the air for a long moment. And smoke masking or not, the flash of these monstrous weapons was almost blinding, not a problem when there's no human at the controls. But now, Crunch felt like he was staring right into the sun.

All this in just two seconds. A second after that, he was roaring over the island, flying so low, the tail of his air beast clipped the top of a date tree on his pull out. If there had been any anti-aircraft fire during his strafing run, he didn't feel it.

When he was able to look back over his shoulder, he saw he'd carved a path of fire and destruction right across the middle of the island, up and over its spiny mountain range and onto the beach below. Anything that had been in his field of fire was simply gone. Trees, missile launchers, people. Just a two second burst and there was nothing left.

Crunch had been a combat pilot for more than 25 years.

He'd never seen anything even close to this.

Hunter went in next.

He'd done this before now—twice. He hit his masking switch, and waited a few seconds for the smoke screen to make its appearance.

Once cloaked, he pushed the main trigger. He knew well now the kick of the four GAUs going off, that floating feeling and then next thing you knew, you were over the target, or what was left of it. His aim-and-shoot spot was just a little south of Crunch's strafing run. Just like his longtime friend, he'd carved a huge swath of flame and smoke across the island, obliterating everything in his path, with no anti-aircraft fire to be seen.

He pulled out and to the left, and then looked at what he'd done. He was not triumphant, not impressed by his actions. Just sort of blank inside for a moment, at the same time being grudgingly respectful of the gargantuan four-gun weapon under his feet.

But still, he was feeling uneasy.

Silkworm missiles were still rising up from the northern end of the island. Not nearly as many as before, but their unknown enemy wasn't giving up.

They seemed to have an unending supply of the weapons too, despite what had to be a huge loss of life among its missile crews and destruction of their launchers. But that too was secondary at the moment. The battle itself was very strange with one side firing dozens of missiles when two or three would usually do, and firing them at a target that for all they knew they'd already sunk and doing it with no anti-aircraft fire, no defensive systems at all that he could see.

Hunter kept thinking over again and again: *This was just not the way you do it*.

His radio crackled to life. It was Ben Wa. His squadron of Su-34 attack planes was incoming, and half the carrier's CAP planes were behind him. Twenty-four planes would soon be in the tight airspace and pummeling the island as well.

Also arriving were the naval copters that had dropped off Crunch to take over the second gunship in Istanbul. They were very low on fuel, but were still able to sink a few of the missile boats in the island's harbor, before finally heading back to the carrier.

It was all over just five minutes later. One strafing run each from nearly 30 aircraft combined. The island was now totally aflame as was the surface of the water in its inlet bay.

It was a lot of destruction—and loss of life, done by their hands. And they still didn't know who this secret enemy was.

But clearly they were not two bit pirates, looking to charge a toll for crossing their lake. Like the people on Corsica, they were well-equipped, there had to be a lot of them and they had to be well-funded.

But by who?

In this crazy world, where some Big War survivors were famously wealthy despite the apocalyptic conditions around them, only a few could afford to outfit an army like this. Whether they earned it, stole it or inherited it, money was still power these days, even more so than before.

Factor in who might want the United Americans to fail in their quest for the six bombs, and only one name came to mind. Then he realized there might be someone close by who could answer that question better than he.

Hunter turned the big plane over once again, much to Tony 3's discomfort.

"I wonder," he said to himself, "when they're going to read Viktor's will?"

His radio crackled to life again. It was a general call from the *USA* reporting a combination of the carrier's defensive capabilities working together had shot down all of the missiles that came close to the ship and were considered a threat. Dozer reported several near misses early in the attack, but also that a lot of the Silkworms fell short and a few blew up in mid-air for no reason.

Hearing this was more alarming to Hunter than hearing about the few near-misses on the carrier. Weapons falling short and weapons blowing up prematurely pointed to incorrect fusing of the warhead, confirming their adversary's amateur status.

These guys might have been well equipped and had money in their pockets, but they definitely weren't pros when it came to this stuff. Even their friends back in Corsica were better.

So what was the purpose of all this?

A diversion . . .

But from what?

What was left?

Damn . . .

The Slugboats. The JAWS guys. They had the fifth bomb with them.

Hunter looked at his fuel gauge—and that's when his heart really sank.

He was already running on fumes; they'd be lucky to make it back to the carrier—with no way to help their tiny fleet of tugs.

Chapter Twenty-Two

Hunter was the first person Dozer contacted after realizing the wave of Silkworms was heading for the carrier.

The second person he called was Dominique.

She was down in Secure 9 with Viktoria as she'd been a lot since this voyage across the Med began, helping the good sea witch make some sense of the thousands of cut-up, jigsaw puzzle pieces that were so key to what the Americans were trying to accomplish.

The battle stations klaxon had just started blaring when Dozer spoke to her down in the secure cabin.

It was a quick message. "We are under attack," Dozer told her. "Please take good care of our guest."

That was it. Moments later, she could hear the big ship suddenly come to life. The crew running to their assigned stations, electronic hums rising from defensive weaponry being turned up to high, jets being carried to the flight deck to take off seconds later.

She'd been through things like this before.

But she wasn't too sure about their increasingly fragile special passenger.

As always, Viktoria was lost amongst the hundreds of pieces of paper on the lighted table. She was just reacting to the barrage of klaxons warning of the imminent attack.

Dominique was quickly back by her side. "Someone is shooting missiles at us again," she told her. "It's best that we stay here until it's safe."

But Viktoria suddenly had other ideas. "Stay here?" she asked. "Shouldn't we be up top and helping in the fight?"

"In this case," Dominique replied, "we should leave it to the professionals."

So they sat on the floor, backs against the wall, facing the big purple candle.

"Is it those same awful missiles again?" Viktoria asked her.

Dominique just nodded.

"I just know my mother is mixed up in this," Viktoria said, biting her lip. "Subtle as usual . . ."

At that moment, the first Silkworm to arrive was just one mile from the ship. The carrier's automatic defensive systems went to work, filling the air with SAMs and thousands of rounds from the CIWS Gatling guns. The missile flew into this barrage and was vaporized; it never made it to within 500 yards of the mighty American vessel. Still the shock wave from the explosion rocked the carrier, already being shaken by the worsening weather conditions outside.

"Well, they got that one," Dominique told Viktoria, noticing she was getting nervous. She added: "They'll get the rest, don't worry . . ."

"In my old pirating days, the biggest boat I was on was a glorified yacht," the raven-haired beauty told her. "Our raids were like pleasure cruises. All this steel and people and big guns going off by themselves. This is not for me."

At that moment, they heard the CIWS weapons open up again, followed by multiple small explosions indicating that SAMs were being launched, many no doubt by the Zabiz missileers. This commotion was followed by another near miss and then an even bigger explosion.

Trying to calm herself, Viktoria looked around at the hundreds of pieces of scrap paper and just shook her head. At the moment it all seemed to be in major disarray.

"Oh thank you so much, my father," she said acidly. "Dysfunctional in life, even more so in death . . ."

Another storm of anti-aircraft fire, another near miss, this one by far the closest, followed by a tremendous explosion. It sounded like it went off right outside the hull from Secure 9.

Viktoria jumped a little, Dominique touched her shoulder lightly and said: "Our guys know what they are doing. We'll be okay. You'll see."

Her soft but confident words settled Viktoria's jitters—but only for a moment.

That's when the next Silkworm was hit by AA fire and exploded. It was so close, it seemed to push the huge ship over on its side only to violently right itself again.

Everything in the cabin was suddenly falling and crashing everywhere, the hundreds of pieces of papers went swirling into the air, for a moment causing a mini-blizzard. All the candles went out. And then the lights did too.

Dominique and Viktoria had been thrown together twice in the commotion. Now they were squashed up against a bulkhead wall, in the dark, as the battle raged outside.

"My God, this is my fault," Viktoria cried. "If we sink and all these people on board are lost, it will be because I sent them on this journey. This stupid, foolish journey."

Dominique reached over and by all good luck, found her two fingers softly touching Viktoria lips.

"That is not so," she told her, sweetly but firmly shushing her. "These people have been doing things like this for years. They know their stuff and they're fighting for the right reasons. We'll be okay. Trust me . . ."

There's was a long silence, followed by two more explosions, but these were far off and muffled.

"See?" Dominique said, words floating into the dark. "It's almost over already."

Suddenly Viktoria's arms were around her—and Dominique didn't resist. A moment later, their lips touched and stayed like that for one long romantic kiss.

In the next moment the lights in the cabin came back on.

The two beauties suddenly found themselves eye to eye, pupils wide open and startled. Another moment passed, before another quick kiss.

Then both said at the same time: "Don't tell Hawk . . ."

Chapter Twenty-Three

The Slugboat team leader was Lieutenant Oliver Masto, Ollie to just about everyone.

He was the captain of Slugboat Number 6, more commonly called the 6Boat. It was his first command with the United American Naval Forces, having joined up two years before.

This sort of thing was in his blood. His father and uncles had fought with Hunter back when the whole idea of re-uniting America was just a dream. That's why he was here today. Looking for high adventure and a way to help save his country, so far he'd gotten plenty of both.

He'd been part of the Gibraltar raid and operationally, this one hadn't been expected to be much different: transporting the JAWS guys to and from the Bee-Bo facility, keeping an eye on the skies and the seas while they went to look for the nuke.

He and his crew of seven had a front row seat for what happened at the port. The climax of the show started when the massive water tower came crashing down into the river about a half mile to his north. A quick call from Cook sent him and two other Slugboats heading for it at full speed.

They found the top of the tower in about fifteen feet of water 100 feet from shore. It was from this vantage point that they saw, for the first time, an air beast in action. The remote-controlled plane came out of nowhere, turned sharply over their position, then did its deadly strafing run on who they would come to learn were the Yam-Yams.

Awesome didn't come close to describing what the airplane looked like with all its weapons opened up. Long streams of flames, chaos and smoke everywhere. No wonder they called them dragons.

Exactly what happened above them next, they still weren't sure. Hunter showed up in the UA's acquired air beast and somehow got the first one under control after it decimated the Yam-Yams. That it too might join the UA inventory could only be a good thing.

Masto never wanted to even think about being on the wrong end of such a terrifying aircraft.

The armed tugs were now thirty minutes out from Bee-Bo, and expected to get back to the carrier in about an hour.

One of the ship's Ka-27s naval copters had met them just as they left the Dardanelles and was now riding shotgun for the return trip. The Slugboat fleet was at full power, all systems working, but their crews were anxious to get back to the safety of the largest warship in the world.

The first sign of trouble came via their long-range FM radio. Masto's comm guy was routinely monitoring the carrier's general transmissions and heard the conversation between Dozer and Hunter about the first incoming Silkworm missiles. This information was relayed to the other five tugs and the Ka-27 copter crew and from that moment on, everyone in the little fleet intently followed what was happening on Thira Island.

The back and forth between the pilots and the carrier left no doubt that the Americans had succeeded in obliterating the island. But it seemed everyone involved had the opinion that wiping out the missiles—or basically sinking the entire island—wasn't going to be the end of it. The carrier expended some time and effort destroying what was, in the end, an extremely vulnerable position for their unknown enemy.

Everyone in the carrier group, the Slugboats included, had gone through more than a few rounds of heavy combat in the past few years. They knew there was usually a definite feel to it when it was over and who won or at least prevailed.

The Battle of Thira Island was different. It seemed more an exercise in waiting for the other shoe to drop.

That happened about twenty minutes later. The six tugboats were cruising at high speed to the southwest when their radar started picking up blips on the surface about ten miles to their north.

Masto happened to be in the radio room when the call came in from the 4Boat. It took about thirty seconds for the rest of the Slugboats to turn their radar sets in that direction. In that time the number of blips on the screen increased to twenty. Then thirty.

"What the hell are these things?" Masto asked his radar guy.

The man replied, "My educated guess, sir, large speedboats. Fast attack stuff . . ."

"Not missile boats?" Masto asked. "Not like Corsica?"

The radar guy shook his head. "Not at the speed these things are moving," he said, indicating the cluster of white blips on his green screen. "They're up around 40 knots. Bouncing around. No way are they lugging Silkworm missiles."

Masto thought a moment. "Any idea what they might be lugging?" he asked, watching the number of blips increase to nearly fifty.

"Another educated guess, sir?"

Masto nodded.

"They know we're out here, because they're heading right for us," the man said. "So, by the way they're moving? I think they might be carrying troops. Boarding parties, maybe?"

Masto hurried up top. Captain Cook himself was riding on the 6Boat, the entire JAWS contingent being spread out amongst the six boats. Masto briefed him on what the radars were seeing.

The JAWS CO took it all in and then calmly issued two orders to his men on the boat. One was to get ready to repel boarders and two, to get into contact with the JAWS guys on the other Slugboats and make sure they were ready to do the same thing.

"Pirates?" Cook finally asked Masto.

The tug commander could only shake his head.

"Forty to fifty attack boats at a time?" he replied. "That's a hell of a lot of pirates . . ."

Less than a minute later, using their NightVision goggles, they could see a bare white line appear on the horizon. It was obvious within a minute these were the mysterious radar blips.

But they were mysterious no more.

They were indeed fast attack boats—and they were indeed filled with men in combat gear. Suddenly coming up on the Slugboat fleet's flank was a small army of maybe a thousand fighters.

Meanwhile, the JAWS teams and Slugboat crews combined equaled less than one hundred people. And the attack boats were getting closer.

As a captain, Cook was the ranking officer in charge but there was none of that "I outrank you" bullshit here. He simply said to Masto: "You guys go up high, we'll take the below . . ."

Masto saluted. "Understood sir."

Then Cook asked him: "Glad you signed up, Ollie?"

"Ask me in an hour," Masto replied.

The six Slugboats went into a classic circle formation. Still speeding full-bore, going southwest, they literally circled the wagons to increase their fields of fire.

As they were doing this, the fleet of fast attack boats began splitting up and to no one's surprise, encircled the fleeing tugboats.

The Slugboats waited, holding their fire as the ring of their new enemy's boats tightened around them. They got so close, they could clearly see each boat carried dozens of their new enemy, all equipped with assault rifles and grappling hooks.

But the strangest thing to be seen in the moments before imminent battle, some of the people in the attack boats were dressed like . . . Vikings.

"Who the hell are these guys?" Masto wondered out loud.

There was no heavy weaponry on these mystery boats. No missiles or big machine guns. The biggest weapons the Americans could see were a few RPGs—rocket propelled grenades. Nothing that could actually sink a Slugboat. It was just a lot of armed guys with grappling hooks.

"They want to board us," Masto thought aloud again. "Not sink us."

It was one of those RPGs that commenced the battle, but not in the way anyone expected.

The Ka-27 copter had taken up a position above the circled tugboats, speeding along with them, waiting to see what was going to happen next. Suddenly one of the attack boats broke from the pack and came in close, a man with an RPG standing on its stern. With no hesitation, the helicopter went right for the boat.

But when the man with the RPG realized what was happening, he raised his aim and fired the grenade at the chopper, clipping its tail-mounted rotor blade.

There was a small explosion and the copter began gyrating wildly. Its tail wash caused the enemy attack boat to capsize, its crew never to be seen again.

The copter managed to get some air under it, then issued a Mayday call to the tugs.

"We'll be in the water about three miles straight ahead," was the helo pilot's last message. "Keep an eye out for us . . ."

A moment later someone in one of the other circling attack boats fired an RPG at the 3Boat. It missed wildly, but that's all it took.

The order to open fire was given simultaneously by the six tugboat captains. Suddenly the night sky was lit up by the ferocious and circular barrage from the half dozen Slugboats, firing outward. Ten of the attack boats went up almost all at once.

The Slugboats were able to bring about some serious firepower; probably more than their attackers ever expected. Each tug had a quad-fifty on board. The four giant fifty caliber machine guns were arrayed in a single turret. Each boat also carried two twin-Bofors anti-aircraft guns that when lowered, were just as effective against sea targets. Add to this that each Slugboat had at least seven JAWS team members on board, all of them armed with M-16 Bananas, many of which came with an attachment that fired M-62 hand grenades.

All of this opened up on the raiders at that first moment—and it stayed that way for the next five full minutes. A crazy high speed battle—like something from the Old West except with boats out in the middle of the Mediterranean Sea at night.

But it became madness and then almost ludicrous the more it went on. No NightVision goggles were needed now—the darkness was lit up like day by all the ordnance being fired back and forth, all this while moving at full speed ahead in very choppy seas. The spray from the boats on both sides was almost blinding. Whenever the Americans were able to get an unobscured look at their attackers, they all looked the same in one regard: high as kites and ready to kill something.

After those first five minutes, none of the attack boats got closer than a couple hundred feet; those that did were quickly dispatched by a quad fifty or a Bofors pom-pom gun. This led to both sides pouring fusillades of gunfire at each other at a distance of about 300 feet apart. This really lit up the night with tracer rounds.

But then it slowly became a battle of attrition. Those suckers in the first boats that came close to the Slugboats got themselves shot up and drowned. Many in what might be called a second wave met the same fate. But now, a third ring of boats moved into position. And these boats were almost filled with troops carrying RPGs.

And at this same point, the JAWS guys and the Slugboat crews started slowly running out of ammunition.

At that same moment, another piece of bad news landed in Masto's lap. All at once the tugboat's shared air defense radar went crazy. Bogies were coming right at them from the same direction as the attack boats.

But these were low, about 500 feet off the water and traveling about 200 knots.

Helicopters . . .

They were over them a moment later—ancient-looking Mi-4 Hound eggbeaters but still dangerous with anti-ship missiles and heavy weapons on board.

Now started a new phase of the fight. Crews on the Slugboats opened up on the copters with everything they had. Stinger missiles, quad-fifties, the Bofors pom-pom guns.

Three of the copters were hit almost immediately, slamming down into the dark seas with barely more than a muffled explosion and puff of smoke.

But then the copter pilots started flying smarter, sweeping down on the tugs, firing their weapons and then quickly flying away. It made hitting them or even getting a good sight on them almost impossible.

The battle raged on. But it became even more confusing for two reasons. A mist was rising up from the choppy seawaters and while not quite a fog, it was like they were going full speed with about twenty feet of clear sailing in front of them, but no more. Fearing a collision at 25 knots, the tugs spread out. But then the mist got thicker and within a minute, they began to lose sight of each other.

While this was happening, 1Boat slowed down to a crawl and guided by two safety flares, the crew expertly pulled the two downed Ka-27 pilots out of the water. The boat then opened its throttle again, but it took a while for the engines to ramp up, and at that moment the raiders on both sides of the tug began sweeping it with multiple streams of tracer fire.

A helicopter appeared out of the dark, all kinds of weapons blasting away. But just as it was about to attack 1Boat, it was suddenly gone, blown to bits by a Stinger missile delivered by the 4Boat somewhere out in the mist. The Slugboats were *always* looking out for each other.

But then—near disaster.

The 2Boat got hit by something, possibly a copter rocket, and went absolutely dead in the water, half of it on fire. In less than thirty seconds, the 5boat was there, pulling up alongside the flaming vessel, taking everyone safely on board. But then they had to watch one of the original Slugboats go to the bottom.

A minute after that, the 4Boat was engaged in a fierce running battle with a trio of attack boats. Nearly firing point blank at each other, the tug wound up colliding with the enemy boats and running them over, dooming their crews. But ammunition carried on all three enemy boats blew up on impact, tearing out 4Boat's propellers and a large part of its stern.

The stricken boat started taking on water immediately, but once again, their tugboat brothers came to the rescue. 6Boat had already pulled alongside 4Boat. The crew and passengers from the stricken tug jumped on board and the 6Boat sped up again, all guns blazing to avoid getting tightly surrounded by the water raiders.

Now two Slugboats were gone, and two of the remaining boats were overcrowded. While the Slugboat crews had been in tough positions before, nothing was quite like this.

But then, a ray of hope.

It came at first as a flash of light, way off on the southern horizon.

Suddenly there was another—then another and another. Masto saw them first, but in seconds the entire crew and all the JAWS guys saw them too.

Two dozen jet fighters of some kind were coming right at them.

The first one went over the 6Boat low and fast so the crew could see its type. Long and slender, looking like a design from the 1950s, they were Yak-28s, the Russian built Harrier-like warplane flown by the UA's staunchest allies, the Flying Knights of God. True to form, they'd come to rescue and not a moment too soon.

Masto had seen the Knights in action before. Prior to nuking Tokyo Bay, the UA conducted a cruise missile strike on a few critical pre-bomb targets in the city's harbor. The UA's submarine the USS *Fitz* conducted those missile strikes and Masto had been a crew member on the Slugboat selected to provide security for the massive u-boat.

But then things went sideways and the sub was attacked by literally hundreds of kamikaze jet airplanes. It was the Flying Knights who came to the rescue that time as well, driving off the suicide bombers and saving both the sub and Masto's Slugboat at the same time.

They'd flown with such admirable precision that day—and that's what they started doing now.

The Yak-28 was a VTOL aircraft. It could take off and land vertically. But it could also control its speed by manipulating its exhaust tubes all the way up to the point of being able to slam on the brakes completely and suddenly stop in mid-air.

The Knights called this "puffing."

Instead of chasing the copters around, a Yak pilot would simply come to a screeching halt and let one of the enemy gunships fly into his field of vision. A two or three second burst from its twin 50 machine guns and the copter was instantly a flaming wreck. Then the Yak would adjust its nozzles again and streak away in normal horizontal flight.

But the Knights were performing these very complicated maneuvers in such a coordinated, almost syncopated way, to Masto and the others it looked like one very large, but very real computer game.

It was the same treatment for the attack boats. The Yaks would wait down near the water's surface and whenever an attack boat streaked by, a barrage from the jump jet would put an end to them in short order.

In this very methodical way, they began clearing the skies of the helicopters as well as firing nearly point blank at the attack boats.

It was a weird kind of controlled pandemonium for about a minute and then everything just stopped. All the copters had been shot down or sent fleeing. Those remaining attack boats backed off and hid themselves in the darkness.

But then, a problem: In the latest bit of chaos, the four remaining Slugboats got separated. Made aware of the situation, the Yaks helped look for the stray tugs, hoping they could corral them all back together again.

After about 10 minutes, they'd found the 1Boat, the 3Boat and the 5Boat. All of them dangerously overcrowded but afloat.

But the 6Boat was still lost . . .

Masto was up in the tug's control house, firing his Banana 16 out the starboard side window, at the same time watching over the crewman who was actually driving the boat.

They were lost in the sudden thick fog, but were still going at full throttle trying to escape any of the remaining attack boats without slamming into something in the dangerous swirling mist.

Cook climbed up into the control house beside him.

"We are getting low on ammo," he told him. "You guys too?"

"Us guys too," Masto confirmed.

Suddenly out of the mist a pair of RPGs streaked by the bridge and struck the rear of the 6Boat. There were two simultaneous explosions and in one moment, the tug's rudder and propeller were destroyed.

The tug began swerving wildly in the foggy, choppy seas, taking on lots of water and nearly capsizing. But then it started to slow down and within a minute, was dead in the water.

Masto and Cook just looked at each other now. They both knew, as everyone on the boat knew, that this was very bad for one very important reason: the 6Boat was carrying the recovered Bee-Bo nuclear mine.

"Time for contingency plans," Cook told him starkly.

Masto was already thinking in that direction.

Like all of the Slugboats, 6Boat had a life raft of sorts aboard. It was an escape pod used by some cargo ships in case they were in danger of sinking. It could be launched off the back of the tug and was lightweight, relatively speaking, but also airtight.

This was where they put the nuke mine after it was recovered. The thought back then was if they ran into trouble with the weather, they would drop the lifeboat and the crew and the mine itself would have a chance to survive. They never thought they'd have to use it in the midst of a battle, but here they were, dumping the thing they'd come so far for.

The 6Boat was bobbing in the choppy water, its crew and the JAWS troopers still firing at several attack boats who were beginning to close in on them. But a large part of the damaged stern had fallen off and the Slugboat was sinking fast.

Suddenly out of the mist, all guns blazing, came the 1Boat. There wasn't enough time to even think about it. Even as it arrived down near the burning stern, the first attack boats had grappled onto the front of the tug and the doped up gunmen were beginning to climb on-board.

Now it got personal. It was wild hand to hand fighting on the deck of the 6Boat. The attackers numerous but obviously hopped up and not coordinated or even highly trained. Still, it was a struggle for the Americans as the attackers' overwhelming numbers gradually pushed them to the rear of the sinking boat.

Within thirty seconds just about everyone on 6Boat had evacuated to 1Boat—all except Cook and Masto. With their backs to the burning stern, Masto pulled the escape pod's handle and the weird-looking lifeboat, with its nuclear cargo, quickly drifted away.

Then, fighting to the very end, both men were about to leap onto the 1Boat when the last enemy helicopter taking part in the battle swooped in and fired two missiles at their already burning tug.

The vessel was blown sky high, along with everyone still onboard. Within seconds, all that remained was a cloud of smoke and some flames on the water.

But then they too faded and were blown away by the wind.

Zig Zigurson was a wanted man, with a price on his head of more than a thousand bags of silver.

He was a mercenary fighter pilot out of Scandinavia, a notorious killer who flew a vintage MiG 21. He'd been the scourge of northern Europe in the post-war years known as much for his cruelty as for his piloting skills.

If some nefarious entity needed an innocent civilian target fire bombed in the middle of the night for no reason other than intimidation purposes, Zig was the one you called.

With his shaven head, tats head to toe and pointed steel implants for teeth he looked like some kind of Angel of Death from a bad drug trip. The name of his warplane was "The Sweet Smell of Hell."

This mission was a little different. It started with a radio call in the middle of the night recently telling him to gather as many merc pilots like him for a big operation two days hence. The money was huge, especially his cut, even if the exact mission was somewhat nebulous.

But now here they were. A dozen jet fighters—MiGs, Mirages, Viggens—even a couple really vintage Luftwaffe F-104 Starfighters. Zig had scraped the bottom of the barrel for this lot, but it didn't matter. His mysterious employers kept telling him this would be a milk run for him and his friends. Blow up a few tugboats, make sure no one is left to tell the tale, then fly home and collect the scratch. Basically getting paid to stuff everything. Zig loved it when the orders were simple.

He could see some kind of something happening below him, lots of smoke and fire on the choppy seas. Naval combat is for chumps, he thought as he radioed the rest of the flight. He could see the tugboats down there that their boss for the day especially wanted sunk. That's what they were here for.

So, he simply said: "Follow me . . ."

Then he pulled back on his throttle and began to dive.

But in the next instant . . . Zig's whole universe turned upside down. His mission contract said that no real opposition was expected, wording that Zig took to mean it would indeed be a milk run.

That dream was dashed in that moment because suddenly he saw a flash of light coming out of the south. And a moment later that flash turned into the last airplane Zig wanted to see—now or ever.

It was Hawk Hunter's unmistakable F-16XL. Cranked arrow wings, six cannons in the nose, multiple Sidewinders underneath, with red white and blue splashed on it everywhere.

The Wingman was suddenly amongst them.

One, two, three of Zig's guys went down in flames in an instant. Then a fourth, a fifth and a sixth.

Zig could plainly see the XL spiraling itself through his group, its nose alight with six cannons firing at once. Every single round hit something, nothing was wasted here, no movement was off even a bit. It was unreal just to watch it. Zig had heard of Hunter of course—at this point who on the planet hadn't? But he'd never seen him in person, in action. But here he was, the famous Wingman, right in their midst.

Zig immediately knew he had to get away. No one signed up for this. But as the flight began to scatter, in a weird way it just made the XL's job easier. With more freedom of movement it was able to pick off the fast retreating jet fighters at an almost leisurely pace. When the cannons weren't quite right range-wise, the Wingman would simply drop a Sidewinder or two and then carry on the close-in fight. It took a little longer but those air-to-air missiles always found their mark.

Always . . .

His short-lived milk run blown to the winds, Zig put his MiG-21 into a tight turn desperate to leave the scene as quickly as possible.

That was not to be however. Just then he saw that his former colleagues were being shot down in the distance by a flight of Su-34s that had been following Hunter. Then he realized someone was right on his tail.

He had only a moment to see the red white and blue as kaleidoscope colors over his shoulder. But it was enough to know that the Wingman himself was on his 6 o'clock, just micro-seconds before firing at him. Suddenly Zig's life began flashing before him—all the atrocities he'd committed, all the misery he'd brought to others, all the innocent people he'd wantonly killed, either for money or a few times just out of boredom.

All of that flashed before him as he felt the dozens of cannon shells rip through his plane and then his body.

The MiG disintegrated and Zig found himself blown out of the cockpit, his flight suit on fire, his parachute nothing more than a cloud of embers. Falling fast, and in unbearable pain, he screamed the whole way down.

The morning finally arrived.

The battle was long over, but Slugboat 3 had yet to leave the scene. The others had sailed back to the carrier, this time with the Yaks riding shotgun low and a flight of Su-34s flying high cover above.

The 3Boat stayed behind for just a few last minutes, hoping against hope to find any survivors from the terrible fighting the night before.

Just as they were about to leave, one of the lookouts spotted a speck way out on the horizon. It looked like a person waving to them. They opened up full throttle and headed in that direction.

Once the person came into view, the crew and passengers of 3Boat couldn't believe what they were seeing.

It was Ollie Masto, swimming towards them. Belt buckle in his mouth, he was pulling the injured Captain Cook and the lifeboat containing the waterlogged but still intact nuclear mine behind him.

PART THREE

Chapter Twenty-Four

Batu Khan and his bodyguard Tuk had no idea how long they'd been prisoners of the United Americans.

After being captured on Corsica, they were bound, blindfolded and flown to the mighty USS *USA,* where they were put in the ship's brig. Located on 11 Deck, it was the very bottom of the boat and was a typical Russian design: a 10x10 compartment with bars on the door. No windows, no water, no lights.

Once alone, and in the pitch dark, Khan had nervously made Tuk swear an oath of silence to him. No matter what awaited them, Khan had told him—beatings, electric shocks, water-boarding—no matter what their captors chose to do to them, they could not say a word about anything having to do with attacking the *USA* or the *Black Widow* would haunt them forever.

Tuk agreed.

After about an hour inside the cell, two UAIA Spooks came to talk to them. They removed their blindfolds and explained they really had only one question to ask: Why did you attack us?

Khan and Tuk said nothing. The Spooks continued asking the same question and in several different ways, but the wall of silence held. No matter, though. After about ten minutes, the Americans nonchalantly picked themselves up and left, double bolting the brig door behind them.

Convinced that beatings, electrical shocks and other kinds of torture were imminent, Khan again lectured Tuk on why it was more important now than ever that they say nothing when their interrogators returned. Stay strong, Khan told him. And keep your mouth shut.

Once again, Tuk reaffirmed his loyalty to him.

So they sat side by side, in the dark room, waiting for a little peek of the Hell they were sure was coming their way.

That had been two days ago.

Nothing ever happened. No one returned to question them, beat them, shock them.

Or feed them.

With no sunlight as a guide, the prisoners lost track of time. To them it seemed like they'd been locked up for at least a week and that the Americans had forgotten all about them.

That all changed that evening.

It started with the sudden and frightening sounds of a sea battle erupting just outside the carrier's hull. It was a bombardment of some sorts, with dozens of explosions going off and what seemed like a lot of near-misses. In the middle of this, they heard a massive launch of the carrier's airplanes, roaring off the deck, two and three at a time, for what seemed like hours. The noise was deafening.

It was a terrifying episode for the prisoners, convinced they were about to be blown apart, in the dark, in the water, a long way from home. The commotion stopped as suddenly as it begun, but after ten minutes of relative quiet, another group of airplanes took off. These were so loud Khan and Tuk had to block their ears even though they were literally at the bottom of the boat. About a half hour after that came the sounds of that very same large group of aircraft landing back on the carrier.

Just minutes after they heard the last plane set down, the door to their cell suddenly opened. A light came on somewhere and three men walked in.

Khan and Tuk were sitting with their backs against the wall in the far corner of the room. At first the light blinded them and they thought—this is it. The Inquisition had arrived. Mouths shut, eyes closed, hearts beating, get ready to take the pain.

But they were puzzled at the same time. Though undoubtedly high up in the command of the monstrous aircraft carrier, at first the three men looked like they were wearing costumes. Like actors from a pre-Big War action film, or maybe a low-budget science fiction movie, everything looked a little too broad, too exaggerated, even too colorful.

One man was wearing a bright blue camo naval commander's uniform with a name tag identifying him as "Dozer." There was no doubt he was in charge. A second man was in bright green naval aviator overalls, name: "Crunch." Big rugged guy, big handle bar mustache, he was what Khan always imagined a real American cowboy would look like. He seemed more threatening than Dozer, but not by much.

The third man was in a flight suit, still wearing his oversized crash helmet which was painted in luminous pearl white with lightning bolts on each side. Even in this dark and awful place, it was sparkling.

The man named Crunch came right up to Khan, stood over him for a moment, then with one hand, grabbed him by the neck and roughly brought him to his feet.

"The ship's captain is in the room," he growled at Khan. "Show some respect . . ."

Seeing this, Tuk immediately jumped to his feet.

"And you," Crunch addressed the bodyguard. "You don't speak until you're spoken to, get it?"

Tuk nodded enthusiastically. He got it.

At that point, the third man took off his crash helmet and pushed back his long hair.

Khan took one look at him and groaned.

"Oh God," he whispered. "It's the freaking Wingman..."

Crunch stepped a few feet to his right, took hold of Tuk by his shoulders and without a word, dragged him from the room.

"Don't forget your vow!" Khan yelled after him.

Dozer slammed Khan back against the wall. "You tried to sink my ship," he seethed at him. "*That's* going to be hard for me to forget..."

Khan did his best to look anywhere but at Dozer.

"Do you know how the Russians used to punish people on this ship?" Dozier went on. "They'd strap them to the number one catapult and send them out for a swim—at a hundred and twenty miles an hour."

Dozer got right in the warlord's face. "Hope you brought a bathing suit..."

A very tense few seconds passed before Dozer glanced at Hunter and asked: "You got this?"

Hunter just nodded. "I got it..."

Dozer slammed Kahn against the wall one more time and then walked out, leaving the warlord alone with the Wingman.

Hunter indicated Khan should take a deep breath and sit. The warlord slid back down the wall and into his original position.

Hunter got down on one knee, laying his crash helmet aside.

"We know you're in league with someone who's trying to stop our mission here and *that's* why you attacked us," he began simply. "It's not complicated. You guys used Silkworm missiles against us—or tried to—on Corsica. And we figured no big deal, really. We've seen two or three in our travels. But you must have heard the racket outside a little while ago? That was a little dust-up with someone else's army and they were using Silkworms too, lots of them, just like you guys. Can you see why that makes us suspicious?"

Khan shifted uneasily but remained silent.

Hunter went on: "Look, whatever you're mixed up in, it's not working. We embarrassed you at Corsica, we just destroyed an island full of Silkworms plus we just sank a fleet of attack boats off the Dardanelles, driven by people who looked like Vikings . . ."

Khan shifted uneasily again. That idiot Sven-Sven, sending his own guys out, in a sea battle, dressed like fucking Vikings.

"But what we don't know," Hunter continued, checking his watch, "is who else is involved and who's running this show. And we really need to know that quickly. So, I can guarantee you this, if you help us now, it will go a lot better for you in the near future. You know, maybe you won't need a bathing suit."

But Khan just stared at the floor. He was cold, he was very hungry and very, very thirsty. But there were good reasons he wasn't going to talk. The repercussions in all situations would be astronomical. He wanted more than anything for this thing to be over. But the consequences of snitching were hard to swallow.

But it was almost as if the Wingman could read his thoughts.

"You know, if you think you and whoever else got involved with you are the only ones that this mysterious puppet master talked to, you're fooling yourself," he said.

He told him the short version of the Philistines at Tangiers. Khan had never heard of them and that was Hunter's point.

"There are a lot of guys like you running around out there," he told Khan. "Trying to do someone's bidding for a huge cash prize, I'm sure. But think about it. Why do you think you and the Viking wannabes and whoever else was there when you made the deal are the only ones this mysterious person is trying to suck in? You didn't know about the Philistines and they didn't know about you. If it's who I think it is running this show, they've got a lot of strings out there, pulling them in all directions."

That was the moment Khan almost said something, but somehow he stopped himself. They sat there in silence, no noise, no movement but the rocking of the ship and Hunter constantly checking his watch.

Then, a knock at the door and one of the most beautiful women Khan had ever seen walked in. She was blonde and divinely gorgeous. Khan knew Hawk Hunter had a long-time girlfriend, named Dominique. She was almost as famous as he was. Khan wondered if this was her.

She leaned down and whispered something in Hunter's ear. Hunter took a moment to let it sink in and then thanked her. She smiled and left.

Hunter picked up his crash helmet and turned back to Khan.

"Well, you had your chance," he said, getting up to leave.

"What changed?" Khan asked, shakily.

"Your bodyguard told us everything we need to know," Hunter replied with a shrug.

Khan was immediately flustered. "I don't believe that," he said.

Hunter shrugged again. "Well, I guess you don't have to. But you treat him like crap, so why wouldn't he turn on you?"

"How do you know how I treat him?" Khan demanded.

"Because he just told us," was Hunter's reply. "They're back there now with him, writing it all down. Everything about Viktor's widow, the Silkworms, and how you made a separate deal with her to screw over the others when this is all over—and then when you got caught, you snitched on everyone else to us."

Khan just glared at him, still amazed he was talking to the famous Wingman, but furious at the conversation. He didn't make a deal with anyone during the operation other than the Red Flags pirate gang. And he had not snitched on anybody.

But he knew the game.

Another few seconds of silence. Khan bit his lip so hard, it began to bleed.

"Here's what's going to happen," Hunter said, heading for the door. "You're not going for a swim, so don't worry about that. What you might worry about is after we drop you off somewhere and word gets around that it was you who told us everything and you who made deals behind your partners' backs.

"Now the best case scenario is you'll just go broke and you'll become a street person, begging people to help you. Worst case scenario? Well, maybe you'll want to take that swim after all."

Khan felt like his head was about to explode. How had he managed to get himself in so much trouble in such a short amount of time?

He spoke again, trying very hard to keep it together.

"I did not make any separate deal with her," he said, knowing he had to at least go on the record as having said that. "Yes, she gave us the Silkworms to sink you because you were looking for these six nuclear devices and she wanted to get to them first, or to most of them anyway. And yes, there was a promise of $200 million in gold. But again there were no separate deals with her, no plans to screw anyone over. If something like that got out, I wouldn't last two days no matter where I was."

Hunter held out his hands like there was nothing he could do, then he opened the door, but not to go out. Instead he let someone in.

Khan was amazed to see the absolutely beautiful blonde walk back in the room with an equally gorgeous raven-haired woman. They were both wearing matching, very tight combat suits. Sexy but dangerous.

Right behind them, eating from an enormous bowl of stew, was Tuk. He and both girls were all smiles.

Khan took one look at his bodyguard and shouted at him: "You coward—you not only talked to them, you lied to them as well!"

Suddenly Tuk straightened up to his full height, which was nearly six-foot-five. His face turned to stone. He glared at Khan.

"Screw you," he told the warlord. "They tricked you. I didn't tell them a damn thing. They just brought me up top to get a bowl of stew. And it tastes fantastic."

Inside the SPOOC, a number of techs and analysts were sitting around the lighted table watching the goings-on down in the ships brig via a closed circuit TV camera hidden in the light socket.

Khan had just buried his head in his hands, realizing he'd fallen for the oldest trick in the book. Lie to both sides, see who cracks first. Only this time there was just one person they had to lie to, and that was him.

Now, in exchange for a promise not to turn him loose on the world like a lamb to the slaughter, he told them everything: about being drugged and taken to the unknown hilltop. Being drugged again and whisked to the Ekranoplan. Talking to the one and only *Black Widow*.

He also confirmed what they really didn't want to know: That Viktor's psychopathic wife had been trying to recover the six hidden nuke mines too and that she had photocopies of the same scraps and drawings they had, and was obviously trying to piece them together as well.

"It sounds like Sven-Sven is no longer a factor," they heard Khan say via the closed-circuit TV. "And clearly my army is out of the picture. So, for me, the only person that leaves is Crazy Norman of the Goth Army, which has about 50,000 soldiers. That guy's a psycho. He's almost as bad as The Black Widow herself."

It all sounded intriguing and important to the people gathered around the lighted table inside Spookytown. But it was also clear that Viktor's wife didn't know where the last remaining bomb was, because she would have recovered it by now.

But neither did they

And at that moment, the deadline for it detonating was less than a day.

Chapter Twenty-Five

Somewhere deep in the bowels of the huge Ekranoplan, appropriately named *Pautina*, "Spider's Web" in Russian, there was also a small dark room, with no windows and a heavy door. But it had no bars. They weren't needed because this was not a jail cell. It was a death chamber. That's why there was a drain in the center.

Two women were down here now, piano wire around their necks, slowly being garroted to death. They had chains on their hands and feet and they were chained to each other. They were the last two women from the group who'd been abducted and forced to reassemble the bad-quality photo copies Viktor's wife had of her daughter's youthful drawings.

But they had not been able to solve anything under the Black Widow's shrinking deadline and now they were about to pay the penalty—very painfully.

The Widow was on hand as were several of her enormous goons/bodyguards. She was not happy. She'd expended lots of time, effort, energy and funds to stop the Americans—or at least slow them down—and she'd failed, miserably.

In the end she'd placed too much faith in all the kidnapped women and that's why these last two had to go.

She took one last look at their final, frantic effort to piece something together from the photo-copied scraps. To her and just about everyone else in the room, it showed no more than three very sharp-peaked mountains—in the middle of a very large city.

They'd scoured maps looking for a city somewhere around the Med that might have three mountains near it, or maybe settlements around a trio of peaks, but there simply weren't any, anywhere.

She gave a nod to the two goons who'd been slowly strangling the women. It was time to go, time to think of something else.

The men had just begun their final twists when in her last breath one of the women gasped: "Maybe they're not mountains . . ."

The Widow held her hand up, stopping the execution at least temporarily.

She pulled on her chin and thought aloud: "Maybe they're *not* mountains . . ."

Chapter Twenty-Six

The carrier was running out of coffee.

That was the bad news Hunter had to face when he went down to the starboard galley after leaving the brig, hoping a fresh pot was waiting for him there. But he found a note instead, informing him of the situation. Coffee was so low, it had to be rationed until further notice. More bad news, the ship was also out of bennies. For Hunter, this was like shutting down Disneyland on his birthday.

There was nothing else he could do now but... actually go to sleep.

But, falling asleep was definitely not part of the plan. The plan was to do everything possible to locate the sixth and final mine in the next eighteen hours or so.

Still he was practically out on his feet by this time.

"Why don't you just try the forty winks thing for a change?" Dozer had told him at the time, asking Ben and JT to get him to his cabin. "They say you feel a lot better afterwards." Hunter finally agreed, but only grudgingly.

Delivered to his door, he tripped into his dark quarters and fell face first onto his bunk. The trouble was his mattress was rolled up in the corner. He hit his temple on the side of the head board which was actually a piece of raw un-brushed Russian steel, knocking himself out cold.

It was odd because he saw nothing but green at first. Green lights, green mist, green stars. Then everything started to clear and he felt a warm wind blowing on his face. He cleared his eyes and found himself standing on a high cliff looking out on a vast ocean that definitely had an emerald sheen to it.

The sky was bright with two suns and he could see a gargantuan ring, like around Saturn, cutting through the daytime sky at a 70-degree angle. Around him were flowers and plants of vivid, unusual colors. Odd but also incredibly beautiful

The wind was swirling around him for a moment. An instant later it shut down to nothing. Then two beams of light appeared in front of him.

And suddenly, there she was. His ghost.

His beautiful, strawberry blonde ghost.

She smiled at him in a way that he felt his chest fill with . . . with something indescribable. It happened anytime he had one of these encounters with her.

Only then did he realize she was dressed differently than ever before. Usually when he saw her she was wearing a full length cape with a hood—that or a flannel shirt and jeans.

But at the moment, she was wearing some kind of super hero costume. Head to toe, tight top, cape, super tight tights and knee high boots.

Supergirl . . .

The second beam of light finally came into focus—and now Hunter was absolutely shocked.

It was Viktor.

Still in the burnt tatters of some kind of uniform, he looked despondent, shriveled, pale as hell and seemed to have a thousand little bleeding sores all over his body. He looked very dead.

The ghost nudged him.

"Tell him," she said firmly.

"Tell me what?" Hunter finally managed to speak.

"Where the last mine is," she said, nudging Viktor again.

"On top of the Great Pyramid," he said in an almost indecipherable rasp. "In Egypt. That's why it's so hard to find."

Hunter stood completely still for a moment. They'd suspected somewhere near the Suez Canal but this was so . . . specific. And about 150 miles away from that waterway.

Astounded by the whole thing, Hunter turned to his ghost and said: "Is this really happening?"

She smiled again and her face became radiant.

"Oh my God," she said, touching his cheek with her hand. "*None* of this is really happening . . ."

Less than a minute later, Hunter was running through the passageways of the ship heading to the deep stern. He went through the three security stations at high speed, holding his security card in front of him. Finally he burst into the Secure Deck 9.

It was dark except for one very large candle.

Viktoria was sitting in the middle of the lighted floor. Dominique was next to her. They were both down to t-shirts and underwear and looked like they too had been up for the last week or so.

He was out of breath but managed to say: "I might know where the sixth bomb is . . ."

Only then did he see that siting between them on the lighted floor were three tiny shapes they'd made from the pieces of the one drawing they had left.

Painstakingly fastened together with tape, glue and paperclips—it must have taken them hours to complete. That was strange enough. But then he realized the trio of 3-D shapes was actually three pyramids, one bigger than the other two.

"So do we," Dominique told him.

Chapter Twenty-Seven

The USS *Mike Fitzgerald* was off the coast of Seattle when it sent the urgent message to the USS *USA* half way around the world.

Better known as the *Fitz*, the giant Ohio-class submarine was two football fields long and weighed more than 17,000 tons. It was originally built to launch barrages of nuclear-tipped ICBMs against America's pre-Big War enemies. At one time, it carried more megatonnage of explosive power than all the bombs dropped in every war in history.

But now it was a versatile underwater super weapon thanks to its owner, super-Irishman Mike Fitzgerald. His majestic submarine was a major part of the United American Naval Armed Forces. Just as the USS *USA* was America's big fist sailing above the waves, the *Fitz* was the second half of the one-two punch, sailing silently below.

When the Mediterranean crisis began, it was decided the sub should maybe stay in the Pacific, where it had been since the Battle of Tokyo Harbor less than two months before. The idea would be to keep an eye on

America's newly-freed West Coast while the mighty carrier was busy in the Med attending to other affairs.

But Fitzie's intel gathering capability on the sub was substantial. So much so, they'd been able to keep an eye on things in the Med as well by tapping into one of the few remaining working spy satellites still circling the globe.

In this way it had tracked the carrier as it had moved eastward, looking for Viktor's nuclear mines. Fitz had also been in close contact with his old friend, Bull Dozer, who provided updated briefings on the carrier's activities several times a day.

On this day, the sub's satellite watch was changing and in the turnover of the real-time satellite images, both the incoming and off-duty techs saw the same thing. They immediately sent the still photos to Fitz and he was just as quickly on a secure sat-phone, that for some reason they called Tomato Cans, calling the carrier.

After Dozer confirmed they were about 200 miles west of the port of Alexandria, Egypt, Fitz broke the news to him: "We've got multiple high-speed vessel traffic just south of your position."

" 'High-speed?' " Dozer asked.

"I hate to use the 'E-word,' " Fitz replied. "But's it's got to be a bunch of Ekranoplans. Nothing else moves like that. So we know who those belong to."

"Any estimate on how many?"

"More than twenty," Fitz told him. "Looks like she's moving someone's army into the Egyptian desert. Any idea why?"

"I'm afraid I do," Dozer replied, quickly filling Fitz in on how they suspected the sixth and final mine might be located atop the Great Pyramid at Giza. "Mrs. Viktor must have the same suspicions—and now it's a race to get there."

Their reception was starting to break up.

"Hang in there," Dozer heard Fitz say. "Call me if you need me . . ."

Chapter Twenty-Eight

It was about an hour before sunrise when the clown plane arrived over the Port of Alexandria, Egypt.

The stars were losing their sparkle by now. The moon had set and the sky was getting brighter. The USS *USA* had arrived about 15 miles off Alexandria just after midnight. Once a vibrant crossroads of civilization, the port had been long ago abandoned, its facilities destroyed during the Big War.

But now, Hunter, the Boop jammed between his knees in the crowded cockpit, flying a mile high over the harbor on his way to the Valley of Giza, counted thirteen Ekranoplans tied up in the harbor's shallow waters. He also saw evidence on piers nearby—disengaged ropes, wires and hoses hanging loose—indicating at least that number, and maybe more, had also been in the port but had since departed.

He knew this was Crazy Norman's Goth Army as delivered by the Widow's flying battleships. Their all-black flags were flying everywhere. The roads around the deserted city were now bustling with trucks and personnel carriers, plus more than a few tanks and mobile guns, like howitzers, and lots of troops. In military-speak, for whatever their many faults, the Goths had "pivoted well," that is, picked up from wherever they'd been and moved here to another environment in anticipation of military action, all in less than 48 hours.

The Great Pyramid at Giza was about 130 miles south of Alexandria and Hunter could see Goth Army troop convoys already heading in that direction. Kicking up clouds of dust and moving very rapidly, their lead elements looked to be well on their way to Giza.

"She wants it so bad this time," he thought, looking down on it all, "she's got an entire army going after it for her."

*****

The little plane reached Giza ten minutes later.

Three pyramids rose up from the valley; one much larger than the other two. This was the Great Pyramid, the tomb of the Pharaoh Khufu. Almost 500 feet high and 6,000 years old, of all the places they'd looked for mines, this had to be the strangest.

Why here? Hunter wondered. After determining where the last device was, Viktoria hit her geology books again and found there weren't any mini-fault lines in the area, hardly any fault lines at all. And while they'd suspected a bomb might be located somewhere high up near the Suez Canal, that man-made waterway was more than 100 miles away.

So again, if ecological disaster was the aim, why put it here?

He descended from 5,000 feet to just 500, and like a bug, began flying around the top of the Great Pyramid.

Trying to steer and activate the Boop at the same time, he slowed the little plane to a crawl. Then he managed to open his tiny door and slip the Boop out sideways, trying his best to be careful with what he thought was a delicate instrument.

He needn't have worried. The Boop started beeping and its LED light began burning bright red almost immediately.

He studied the tip of the pyramid through his Night-Vision glasses and saw what looked like a very sloppy cement patch job on the northern side of the pyramid about ten feet down from the peak. The Boop was telling him that behind the poorly applied mortar lay something like a trash barrel and in it, Viktor's sixth and final nuclear mine.

"Wow, are we really this lucky?" he wondered out loud.

His head was still spinning from his dream—or whatever it was—and all the factors that had brought him to this very ancient and mysterious place. Life *is* strange, he thought. If someone told him at the beginning of this adventure that he'd wind up in Egypt circling Pharaoh Khufu's tomb with a hula-hoop on his lap, he would have told them *that* sounded more like a dream than what actually happened.

But here he was, praying that this really was the end of it. Pry this thing loose from the peak, disconnect the detonation cable, and then get out before the Goths even arrived. Viktor's last laugh would fall flat on its face and the world would be just a little bit safer—at least for a while.

Hunter checked his watch. Keeping in mind a number the SPOOC analysts had given him before take-off, at that moment, they had one hour and twenty-two minutes to go before the weapon exploded.

It seemed like plenty of time for what they had to do.

A flurry of radio calls followed Hunter's discovery.

He called Dozer and Dozer called the carrier's command center. The command center then sent a message to the JAWS CO Jim Cook and the recovery team. Having taken off from the carrier about thirty minutes after Hunter, they were at that moment in a holding pattern orbiting a mountain near Tanta, Egypt, about 30 miles northeast of Giza.

War of Dragons

This time the team was made up of six Hind troop-carrying gunships with six JAWS guys in each, plus a single Ka-27 naval copter with the JAWS engineers and their equipment. Cook radioed back an acknowledgement and Dozer called Hunter with the message: "They'll be there in ten minutes. Loop us in when you make visual contact with them . . ."

Hunter rogered that, then turned north and climbed. Back up at 5,000 feet he spotted the dust trails of the approaching Goth Army now about 50 miles away. That put them about an hour outside Giza. He checked his watch. The nuke was supposed to detonate in a little less time than that. It was going to be close, but the UA knew how to do this kind of thing because they'd done this kind of thing so many times before.

Hunter went back to circling the pyramid, keeping note of the plumes of dust being caused as the Goths got closer. But then he spotted seven specks in the sky—it was a beautiful sight. The recovery team was here.

He was about to call Dozer to confirm visual contact when he felt a troublesome buzz coming from somewhere deep inside him.

This was not good . . .

Suddenly, his internal early warning system was burning as hot as the Boop had been earlier.

He began climbing once again, looking in all directions for the source of this disturbance. Finally something off to the south caught his eye, emerging from the fading darkness.

Smoke first, then the clouds of dust. Then troop trucks and tanks. Hundreds of them.

Another army?

Who the hell are these guys?

He pushed the clown plane's throttle to the max and steered due south. By using the zoom function on his specially-adapted NightVision goggles, he was soon able to pick out individual vehicles, weapons and finally troops. He was stunned by what he saw.

All the troops were wearing those same crazy silver helmets as the Philistines back in Tangiers.

"Philistines 2.0?" he wondered, really questioning the reality of all this now. Their murderous cohorts had been turned into fiery bones and dust back in Tangiers. Was this their way of getting revenge by seizing another "hidden treasure"—as in another 3.5 kiloton nuclear bomb? And how did they know it was even here?

Whatever the case, a second army of at least 30,000 troops and many armored vehicles was about twenty miles south of the Great Pyramid and heading right for it.

But just as he was about to call the ship with the astonishing news, another feeling bubbled up deep inside him. He swung west—only to see a *third* army, just as big if not bigger, heading for the Great Pyramid as well. Smoke, dust clouds and lots of tracked weapons. It was almost a mirror image of the Goths and the Philistines.

He flew over them now and got the biggest shock of all. He could see the emblem on their trucks and tanks. It depicted a crucifix surrounded by flames.

No fucking way . . . he breathed.

Years before, the Americans ran up against a neo-Nazi KKK-affiliated group called The Burning Cross. After a number of fierce engagements the UA threw them out of the country. A UAIA report a few years later said they'd escaped to deep South America and later became a merc outfit.

Now, they were in the Middle East? How? There was only one explanation: the Widow must have offered to pay them too, just as she had the Philistines and The Goths.

"What the hell is going on?" Hunter asked out loud. "Is everyone here for the same thing?"

At that moment, he witnessed yet another remarkable sequence of events. The Philistine army to the south, having spotted the Goths coming from the north, had begun firing at them with some impressive mobile artillery. In the meantime the Goths had spotted the Burning Cross army coming from the west and started bombarding it with high explosive missiles. A split second before the first missile fell, the Burning Cross had opened up with howitzers on the Philistines army in the south. All this had stopped the three armies in their tracks, at least for the moment.

A three way battle...

Three armies, all of them converging on the Great Pyramid.

Pitted against each other to be the first to reach the prize at the top.

The sixth nuclear mine.

Hunter immediately turned north and started heading back to the ship as fast as the clown plane could carry him. He was on the radio at the same time, telling Dozer: "Freeze everything. Change in plans. Tell the recovery team to find a place to land and stay there until they hear from us. I'm on my way in . . ."

Chapter Twenty-Nine

Hunter bounced back onto the carrier twelve minutes later.

The little clown plane was smoking heavily and just barely able to stay airborne when he touched down. He'd run the little engine far beyond its limits and it was squawking loudly in protest.

He was aboard and safe, but there was no time to meet in the War Room. No time to pore over the intelligence and plan the best option. Their cautious, methodical approach had been turned inside out. It was now a full-blown crisis situation.

The Americans' mission was still to recover the mine, but the circumstances had drastically changed. When Hunter first looped around the Great Pyramid they had more than an hour before the mine was due to blow. Back then, they were keeping an eye on the minutes.

But now, with this new major twist, it was every second that suddenly counted . . .

Hunter climbed out of the clown plane and met the carrier's command team right out on the flight deck. Dozer, Crunch, the Cobras, Ben, some Spooks, a couple Flying Knights . . . they were all there. The ship was going to full war footing which meant most of its airplanes would be launched, either to take part in whatever was going to happen at Giza or to stay overhead and protect the carrier from what might lay ahead.

As the carrier's principles were having their hurried conversation out on the deck, dozens of personnel were running by them—pilots, air crews, anti-aircraft gunners. They'd all done things like this before to—called to full alert before some usually intense combat. But that did little to dampen the grim tension of the moment.

They were going to war again.

The conversation on the flight deck became intense. From Hunter's eyewitness account he confirmed that all three armies—the Goths, the Philistines and the Burning Cross—were full of the worst characters on the planet. This meant for certain that their ranks were burgeoning with murderers, rapists, and other dregs of the earth.

"Every freak in the world must want to be there," Crunch said.

No one could disagree with him.

The problem was this bizarre battle that had already erupted might interfere with the UA getting to the mine before it was too late.

They had to get Cook's engineers to the top of the pyramid, somehow protect them while they did their work and at least delay a full-out three pronged assault to seize the pyramid and the nuclear prize it held on its peak.

And they had to do all this in less than thirty minutes—and the clock was ticking.

The air wing was already launching as the command team finished their discussion amid the controlled chaos on deck.

Most of the ship's Su-34 attack planes were going to Giza, as well as the Flying Knights' Yak-38 squadrons. The command's quick plan was radioed to all the pilots. In brief: if needed, the UA warplanes should bomb and strafe positions ahead of all three armies in hope of at least delaying the three sided advance long enough for the JAWS guys to get on the pyramid and do their thing. And while the hope was that their massive show of force might deter the three armies long enough for them to secure the nuke, if any Americans were fired on, then it would be gloves off.

While not exactly a desperate plan, it was definitely something decided while they were in an extreme crisis management mode.

Sure, let's try this, because after that our options are limited.

The meeting broke up with the pilots running towards their aircraft and Dozer returning to the bridge to oversee the all-out launch.

Hunter's F-16XL had been brought up from below during the pandemonium. Engines already started and warmed, it came up on the carrier's enormous center-deck flight elevator with two Su-34s whose engines were also warmed up and ready to go.

Hunter reached his airplane at the same time the crews for the pair of Su-34s reached theirs. Switchblade Steve Ward and Jocko Johnson were right in front of him, climbing into their bird.

"See you at the party," Ward yelled down to him.

Hunter just gave him an exaggerated salute.

"First round's on me," Hunter yelled back.

Then he walked around the front of his XL super-fighter and literally bumped into the crew of the second Su-34.

He was quickly all apologies until he realized the two pilots had actually run into him on purpose. Hunter was confused until the pilot closest to him took off their helmet.

It was Dominique, dressed in full combat flight gear.

Hunter began to say something like this was a bad joke to pull at such a very serious moment . . .

But then he realized it wasn't a joke.

"Please don't tell me that you're going . . ." he started. But her finger was on his lips in an instant, stopping him mid-sentence.

"We'll need all the planes we can send, right?" she asked him.

Hunter had to nod in agreement.

"And you know I know how to fly one of these, right?"

Again, she was right. During their adventure in the Pacific a few months before, they'd taken a side trip deep into Siberia and on the way back, with the controls on autopilot, Hunter fell asleep and Dominique landed the plane on the carrier herself, saying she didn't want to wake him. He also knew she'd been training with Ben Wa's squadron, and had spent much of the time sailing from the Pacific to here, doing all she could to qualify in one of the Americanized attack planes.

And now here she was.

"But this is going to be real combat," he started to plead with her, but she just gave him the eye and a half smile and that stopped him cold.

The flight suit, the helmet, the short hairdo. It was all working in such an incredible way. Did he at all miss the glamourous, regal, outrageously beautiful *blonde dramatique*?

It was a question for another time.

"Just be careful," he finally relented. She shot it right back at him. "You be careful too," she said. "Besides—don't worry, I'll have my guardian angel with me."

Hunter understandably froze at the sound of that—but again it only lasted a moment. He was suddenly distracted by the second pilot who now took off their own helmet.

It was Viktoria, of course.

Hunter almost felt like he was having a flashback to his dream or whatever it was.

But suddenly Viktoria's hand was on his chest.

"Don't worry," she said, also looking outstanding in her combat suit. "I'm in the third-man jump seat."

The joke was complete when JT walked around the tip of the wing and came upon the small, confused group and faked being confused himself.

"What did I miss?" he said with a straight face.

A minute later, Hunter was being hooked up to catapult 2, which was right next to catapult 1 where the two girls and JT were being hooked up as well.

One moment before both steam catapults activated, Hunter looked over at their airplane and saw Dominique looking back at him.

She blew him a kiss.

Then the Su-34 launched, and she was gone.

Chapter Thirty

It was a scene of complete chaos by the time Hunter in his F-16XL superfighter arrived back over Giza.

The sun was up, the sky was filled with smoke, smoke trails and all kinds of heavy ordnance going back, forth and sideways in the bizarre and ongoing three-sided battle.

The recovery team had left their holding spot and the Ka-27 was right now orbiting the peak of the pyramid having already landed two of Cook's guys safely on top. Hunter went by the pyramid just slow enough for him to see the two men trying to break away the poor cement job around the trash can and get to the nuke mine within. The sooner that happened, the better for all of them.

The six Hind gunships were themselves circling the pyramid but farther out, their troops ready to be dispatched where they were needed, which was hopefully, not at all.

To complete the security cone, circling high above at five different altitudes, the air squadrons of the USS *USA* were forming up, also ready to be called on.

The three armies were now within a mile of the pyramid and creeping forward slowly. They were still blasting away at each other, but it was now a true free for all as each side was firing at the other two, at the same time taking two streams of incoming fire themselves.

But just moments after Hunter arrived on the scene, someone in one of the three armies started paying attention to what was happening at the top of the Great Pyramid.

Suddenly some of the firing from the Philistine Army in the south was re-directed at the top of the pyramid, possibly the gunners under the wrong impression that the climbers were from one of the other two armies, now so close to the nuclear mine.

Shooting at a nuclear weapon was never recommended but it was the fact that the JAWS guys had to take cover from the incoming barrage that provoked a reaction from the Americans.

Before he knew he was even doing it, Hunter swooped down on the Philistine army and took out the mobile howitzer that had fired on Cook's guys atop the pyramid.

But at almost the same moment, the Goths began firing at the pyramid as well. Then the Burning Cross army did the same thing.

A moment later all three armies were firing at the Great Pyramid and suddenly the sky full of UA warplanes began to dive. That was all they needed. Swooping in at high speed, they bombed and strafed dozens of offending weapons systems, obliterating them and everything around them.

This was the battle for the first five minutes. Each of the three armies firing on one another as well as taking shots at the people atop the pyramid—whoever the hell they were. In his superfighter, Hunter was screaming above the battlefield in his XL superfighter, dodging all kinds of ordnance, and taking out as many enemy howitzers and missile launchers as he could find, all the while trying very hard not to collide with other friendly aircraft.

War was chaos and this was a good example of it. Hundreds of shells and missiles being thrown back and forth even as the three individual armies were making slow but steady progress towards the pyramid. Every chance he had, Hunter would roar past the tip of the pyramid to see how the recovery process was going—but each time he saw the JAWS guys give him the thumbs-down. He didn't know what the issue was exactly, but something seemed to be wrong with digging the mine out of the crappy cementing job Viktor's minions had done.

Then suddenly, more buzzing in his head. He looked straight up through his canopy to see two chevrons of contrails passing overhead, 20,000 feet up.

He didn't need radar or some kind of internal IFF to know they were Russian-built MiGs. MiG-19s, '23s, '25s, even a few '27s.

Who did they belong to? Were they even at the right battle?

It made no difference. They started peeling off a pair at a time and begin engaging the UA aircraft.

This turned the pandemonium of the battle into complete madness.

Hunter had no choice but to take on the attacking jets—in the wrong location or not, they'd fired on UA personnel. These days, that's all it took.

Now there were two separate battles. One on the ground, still raging fiercely, and one in the air. Between the altitudes of 5,000 and 10,000 feet, the skies were crowded with nearly one hundred warplanes. Hunter found himself roaring through the enormous furball, taking out targets with just a squeeze or two from his nose-mounted six-pack of M61 cannons—at the same time, trying to get a close look at every Su-34 that went by, to see if Dominique and Viktoria were aboard.

It soon became clear though, whoever the other aircraft belonged to—and chances were good that they were just another merc team hired by the Widow in her outlandish attempt to seize the one last nuke—they were terrible dog fighters. They barely knew how to fly their famous Russian MiGs, some of them exploding in flames without firing a shot. The Flying Knights Yak-38s proved to be particularly effective against them, "puffing" when they could and then taking a shot at the enemy plane as it suddenly zoomed by.

Making it even worse for the merc fighter jocks, should one get close to the ground several people in different armies would take a shot at them with a handheld SAM missile, such as a Stinger. Pretty soon the intruders must have realized they were either at the wrong gig or they'd been duped and were wildly outmatched.

Either way, after a full ten minutes of this, those MiGs that hadn't been shot down left the area at high speed, having enough of the madness that had engulfed the Giza Plateau.

But all this had taken time. Hunter couldn't keep track of the minutes during the intense combat. Now looking at his watch he was stunned to see they were down to just seven minutes before the nuke was going to detonate.

He called Cook, who was in the Ka-27 circling the pyramid under intense fire himself while his men worked on getting the nuke out.

"This is tougher than we could have ever imagined." his friend radioed back.

Hunter was mystified. When he did the first recon of the peak he saw a very bad cement job barely holding the garbage can in place.

"The so-called crappy cement job was just another ruse by that a-hole, Viktor." Cook told him. "Not that we should be surprised, but underneath it there's is a triple bolted steel base which in turn is bolted into several large granite anchors which in turn are bolted into the original pyramid stone. To do it right, we'd need twenty guys up here with some fairly heavy equipment and about twelve hours or so."

"How about if we do it wrong?" Hunter replied.

But he wasn't expecting an answer.

Now the moment of truth had come.

Hunter swooped back over the insane battlefield, dodging missiles and AA fire, nearly overwhelmed by the insanity of it all.

Is this what the world had come to? Everyone madly fighting each other just so they could get their hands on a weapon that came very close to ending all life on the planet years ago with the Big War? Or everyone doing the same thing, but just for money?

The three armies were now just a quarter mile or so from the base of the pyramid at which point they would actually slam into each other, creating a battle so huge and so bizarre, it brought to mind something that might happen in the Peloponnesian and Punic Wars. Large groups of soldiers, in this case, none of whom had souls or hearts or consciences, battling each other to the bloody end and taking down as many as they could with them.

All this, with less than five minutes to go before the nuke went off.

They are the worst of the worst . . .

Those were the words running through Hunter's head now. Wouldn't the world be a seriously better place without the dregs like they'd fought off Sicily or the Silkworm shooters in the Aegean or the Philistines near the Tangiers Dam and now here again?

Why jump through hoops just to save the hides of some really crappy human beings in The Burning Cross? Let them live so they could resume terrorizing the planet? Where did the UA's moral obligation begin and end?

There were no innocents anywhere near this place. All that was left were these homicidal losers. Why should the UA drop one bit of blood for them?

Oh, none of this is really happening . . . that's what the angelic ghost said.

Now those words were bouncing around his head too.

Cook got the radio call a few seconds later.

At that moment it seemed nonsensical. So much so, he asked Hunter to repeat it. Twice.

Only then did he understand. As the mission commander, Hunter had the first and last say in everything connected with the mission—and everyone was very happy with that arrangement.

But what he was asking Cook to do now was crazy.

And certainly against the mission orders.

So, it took Cook a moment to get it too.

Then he was all in.

With a wave of his hand, Cook called on the Ka-27s crew to swoop in and pick up the guys atop the pyramid. "Leave the equipment," Cook told them as they all jumped into the copter. Once aboard, it quickly moved away to the north.

As this was happening the skies high above the battlefield suddenly emptied of all UA aircraft. Now all that was left was for the three armies to collide and begin slaughtering each other for the right to claim the nuke.

Hunter was the last to leave.

He put the XL into a straight up climb and didn't level out until he got to the nose bleeding altitude of 80,000 feet, nearly sixteen miles high.

He turned on his long range video cameras and checked his watch. He could see the fighting raging far below and just shook his head.

"No matter what we do," he thought, "this world is always going to be screwed up. That's just the way it is."

He checked his watch a second time and then went back to scanning the battlefield below. Suddenly off to the south a large object came into view. It was flying at about 5,000 feet, heading straight for the pyramid and the three battling armies, trailing a long tail of flames and smoke, its nose lit up like some mythical fire-breathing dragon.

The sixth and final air monster had arrived to protect the sixth and final nuclear mine.

Hunter glanced at his watch again and then simply said: "Right on time . . ."

The nuke atop the Great Pyramid went off a second later.

Chapter Thirty-One

The USS *USA* passed through the Strait of Gibraltar around noon two days later, a strange parade of vessels following in its wake.

Directly behind the massive carrier were the eight surviving Slugboats, two of them under tow. Behind them, five captured Ekranoplans, their various insignia scraped off and the UA's star and stripes roundel put in their place.

Along with the two Z-130s, these were the spoils of war. After the battle at Giza, the Americans picked the five Ekranoplans in Alexandria Harbor that looked to be in the best shape and then destroyed the rest. The sailors whose Slugboats were lost during the Dardanelles operation now crewed these massive flying battleships.

The carrier's immediate destination was New York City. Specifically it was going to the newly re-built Brooklyn Shipyard where it would undergo an overdue refitting which would include extending the ship's flight deck and hull to allow it to better use the pair of Z-130 gunships.

It would take six days to cross the Atlantic and reach Brooklyn.

As they passed through the famous strait, the master of the deck blew the ship's horn four times as a salute.

But there was no one left on Gibraltar to hear it or to wave as they went by.

Dozer was sitting alone in the SPOOC chamber when Viktoria and Dominique came in.

He pulled out two chairs right next to him and asked them to sit down.

Like him, like everyone on the boat, they were weary but very glad that the whole Mediterranean adventure was coming to a close.

"I'm sure we'll have some kind of gathering for the crew at some point," Dozer told them. "But I wanted to talk to you first in a little more of a controlled environment.

Viktoria looked at Dominique and said: "I'm honored..."

Dozer always got down to the brass tacks.

"You helped us out here tremendously." he started out, addressing Viktoria. "But you not only helped us, *you* saved the world—just like your father wanted you to. Or at least he said he did. If it wasn't for you, who knows what would have happened."

Viktoria began to say something but stopped. Never did she think she'd get any acknowledgment or thank you for what just happened. It never once crossed her mind. She did it solely to prevent a planet-wide cataclysmic event.

"We also like how well you meshed in here," Dozer went on, "and how you can understand the determination we have in what we do."

"That much I do understand, sir," she replied.

"So then," Dozer plunged on, "we would like to offer you the position of intelligence analyst here on the ship, your expertise being intelligence gathering and decryption. You'd get clearance and work in Spookytown, and Dominique would be your liaison to the military side of things."

Viktoria just stared back at him. "You want me to *join* you?" she asked, making sure she heard him right.

Dozer nodded and so did Dominque. She'd known about this all along.

Now Viktoria really couldn't speak.

Dozer tapped the top of her hand. "Go on the next deployment with us," he said. "See if you like it . . ."

This time she did take a moment to think of the ramifications of what they were asking. Her father had been one of the worst people ever on Earth. Now, if she joined with the United Americans, she could do something that could really change some of the misery he left behind.

Finally she smiled, got misty, hugged Dozer, then hugged Dominique too.

"I would be proud to join you," she said, adding with a smile. "But I have just one condition . . ."

Thirty minutes later, Ben, Cook, Crunch and the Cobra Brothers were in the SPOOC, sitting around its lighted planning table.

They too were weary and over-worked, but glad to be heading home.

This was a security briefing. Dozer produced a piece of yellow paper with a red stripe running up its side. Classified information was handled aboard the carrier in this manner. Yellow paper plus red stripe meant Top Secret.

"This is the post mission assessment just finished by the Spooks," Dozer began, reading from the report. "We left quite a trail behind us on this voyage."

He passed around a photo taken the day before by Fitz's spy satellite network. It showed the Mermesa Tower in Istanbul, its top two floors ablaze and a large military presence in the streets below.

"They had a coup there two days after our visit," Dozer explained. "One of the Saladin's top dogs seemed to have gotten in some, let's say, 'unexplainable trouble,' and as a result, he and a lot of his boys were sacked. That opened the door for a rival gang to move in and take over. So, if you're keeping score, in the new Turkish

Empire, the Saladins are out, a group called the Otto 2s are in."

He passed around another satellite photo.

"This is the port of Bee-Bo on the Bosporus," he said, adding, "Or what's left of it."

The picture showed the vast port facility utterly destroyed from what had to have been a fire so huge, it actually jumped the waterway and burned down nearly a mile stretch on the eastern side as well.

Dozer explained: "Remember, the Yam-Yams started a big fire down there, then there was what happened when the water tower was blown up and then the auto-piloted Z-130 strafed the place. So, it looks like all that combined to cause all this. Sad really because that place literally was the crossroads between East and West. Now, it looks like the world's biggest junkyard."

Another photo. It showed hundreds of people gathered alongside an icy river near the wreckage of an airplane with snow-capped mountains in the background. Though it was hard to tell, from overhead they seemed to be performing some kind of ceremony.

"This is the River Split," Dozer explained. "And that's the Matterhorn you see behind them. According to some signals intel we picked up, these people were on hand doing a ritual to 'reestablish' the curse of the Matterhorn. We don't know what that means, but we're sure it had something to do with our activities there recently..."

One more satellite photo showed what appeared to be swirling storm clouds hanging over the area around the Tangiers Dam with much of the ground below being blackened.

"Those are actually vultures,' Dozer said darkly. "Thousands of them—maybe hundreds of thousands. They showed up after the Z-130 tore up the first Philistines' camp and I guess because there's so much—ahh, food—around, they've decided to stay. There's so many of them the very few people who lived in the area have fled, I'm guessing never to return. And who can blame them? I mean, that's freaking gross..."

One last photo was passed around.

"And gentlemen," Dozer said, "in case you missed it as we went by, this is the Rock of Gibraltar. As you can see, it looks a little different now."

He was right. The once Great Rock now resembled a large piece of charred firewood, sticking up in the air, still smoking, with any beauty or magnificence the place had once long gone.

The men gathered were astonished by the photos.

Ben spoke for all of them when he said: "We may have prevented people around the Med from having an enormous ecological disaster come down on them. But, at the same time, I don't think we're going to be invited back anytime soon."

Ten minutes after that, Dozer left the SPOOC and walked down to the carrier's media center. He'd just received a message that Tony 3 had something important to show him.

Dozer walked into the room—it looked like a mad scientist's laboratory, if that scientist was into video and especially radio—and found Tony 3, as always, hunched over his video bay. "Thanks for coming, Captain," he said, getting to his feet.

"Is this about those girly tapes I borrowed from you?" Dozer asked him. But the normally jovial Tony barely chuckled at the joke. "I'm sorry sir," he replied, deadly serious. "There's something you really have to see . . ."

Dozer sat down in front of a big TV screen and Tony started his video player.

"Sir, you'll recall what happened back in Tokyo Harbor a micro-second before our nuke lit off?" Tony asked him.

The Americans nuked Viktor's bomb making factory in Tokyo Harbor as a very last resort. But in doing so, they also not so secretly hoped that when their bomb went off, Viktor would be one of its victims.

They'd had him cornered in similar situations before, but he'd always managed to slip away from them—and this time it was no different, at least for a while.

When the UA watched the nuclear explosion in Tokyo Harbor in real time via a TV camera mounted on one of their Su-34s, what they saw was what looked like a large, highly-polished cube rocketing out of the bomb factory just nano-seconds ahead of the nuclear blast. Expecting Viktor would have some kind of escape plan in place this time as well, and recognizing that the weird flying cube was really some kind of escape pod, the UA was ready to chase the strange little object—which they did, all the way down to the South China Sea.

Exactly what it was, they didn't know as the flying cube literally disappeared shortly after it crashed, but Dozer had dreamed about the strange little object more than once since it had happened.

"How could I forget?" was all he said now.

Tony said: "Well, watch this, sir. It's the video Hawk shot of the Giza Pyramid when that nuke went off. I've dialed it down to the slowest-motion possible."

Dozer did as asked, and sure enough, just as the bomb was detonating, something clearly shot up through the peak of the Great Pyramid.

Cubes . . .

Three of them, ascending so quickly, it was almost as if they were using the blast's energy to propel themselves.

"Our old friends, sir," Tony said to Dozer. "Three of them just like the one from Tokyo Bay."

Dozer watched the slowed down tape three more times, but he didn't need further convincing. Whatever had shot out of the Tokyo Bay weapons factory an instant before that nuke went off, three of the same things escaped just an instant before the Giza detonation.

"What the hell are they?" he asked Tony, totally lost for an explanation.

Tony could only shake his head. "Someone above my grade might be in a better position to answer that sir," he said. "But the way they move, the fact that they can survive a nuclear explosion, and might even use it as a kind of power source . . . who knows? But it's something way out there, that's for sure. But maybe that's why the sixth nuke wasn't part of the whole scary doomsday cataclysmic event. Maybe it was there to let these things out. Or escape. Or something . . ."

Dozer could only nod in agreement.

"Who else has seen this?" he asked.

"Just you and me, sir," Tony replied.

"Let's keep it that way for now, OK?" he asked. "Let me talk to Hawk and the other guys about it first."

"Absolutely, sir," Tony replied.

Dozer watched the slowed down tape one more time, then said: "Just when you think nothing more insane could happen, you find out you're dead wrong."

Hunter was out on the stern of the ship, leaning against one of the Flying Knights' Yaks. He was looking out on the wake of the great ship and the strange procession of Slugboats and Ekranoplans following behind.

"Welcome to our bathtub navy," he thought.

JT walked up and joined him. He seemed extremely pleased about something.

"Did you hear the latest?" he asked Hunter, searching his jacket pocket and coming out with a joint.

"Why don't you tell me?" Hunter replied.

"I've had this thing rolled since Tokyo," he said, trying his Bic lighter. "Figure now is a good time to celebrate . . ."

"The news?" Hunter reminded him.

"Me and Crunchie are flying to your friend Viktoria's island and bringing her entire gang of girls back here to the ship. They're going to do the next deployment with us."

Hunter had to smile. He knew Dozer planned to ask Viktoria to join them and he guessed she'd probably want her own little crew to be with her too. But he also knew that for JT, this was literally a dream come true. Viktoria's "crew" was actually a pack of beauties who she turned first into Caribbean pirates and then into special ops soldiers.

"We're taking off in the first Z-130 once we get in shouting distance of Bermuda," JT continued. "Landing there, loading them up and bringing them back here. And I get to show them around the ship."

He finally got the joint lit. He took a very deep drag and let it out slowly.

Then he looked up at the bright blue sky, his eyes beginning to twinkle.

"Wow—a bunch of beautiful amazon pirates coming to stay on the ship," he said woozily. "There *must* be a God . . ."

He passed the joint to Hunter who took two quick hits—his limit—and passed it back.

Then he looked up at the sky too, for a very long time, recounting all the many strange things that had happened during this most recent adventure. Then he thought about Viktoria and Dominique, Chief Zabiz and his guys and what happened at Bee-Bo and Giza.

"Maybe not 'God,' " he finally said. "But Something's out there."

The bright blue Ekranoplan was hidden under the cliffs at La Mac on the northeast corner of Corsica.

The remains of the huge UA attack on the place a week before were still very evident. Everything either flattened or destroyed, many thin pillars of smoke still rising into the air. Devastated or not, though, La Mac was still the best place in the Med to hide a large vessel.

There was a grand cabin deep inside the strange flying boat where the Widow slept on a gigantic round waterbed. She was there now—with a visitor.

He was taking up nearly half the bed and all of the blankets—that's how large an individual he was. There was something about that that excited her.

But...

She threw the blankets off him and hit him once, hard on the head.

Crazy Norman woke up with a start.

"I want to hear it all again," she demanded of him. "And this time, say it like you mean it."

Norman was still recovering from two days of lovemaking and heavy drinking. He loved rum and the Widow loved her vodka.

"Okay." he began, slowly. "I forgive you for kidnapping me that night. I forgive you for misleading me that night. I even forgive you for killing off my army in Giza..."

"Thank you, my love," she replied.

Norman thought another moment, though, then said: "But I have one question: Your husband sent your daughter her drawings in scraps as clues to the nukes' locations. Now at one time in the past you must have had the original drawings, but for this you only had photocopies. Why was that?"

She replied with a question of her own. "Ever wonder why they call me the Black Widow?" she asked him.

He just shook his sleepy head no.

She took an ice pick from under her pillow, put it in his left ear and pushed until it came out the other side of his skull.

"You stupid fool," she told him as the last bit of life flickered from his eyes. "Who do you think tore them up in the first place?"

About the Author

Mack Maloney has written more than 50 novels including the best-selling *Wingman* series and the *Codename Starman* military mysteries, as well as three nonfiction books, *Mack Maloney's Haunted Universe*, *Beyond Area 51* and *UFOs in Wartime*. Mack is also the host of the nationally syndicated radio show and podcast "Mack Maloney's Military X-Files."

Coming Soon!

MACK MALONEY'S

SPOOKY ACTION AT A DISTANCE
CODENAME: STARMAN SERIES
BOOK 4

When Navy Detective Chris Starr is forced into spy rehab after suffering from "black-ops burnout," he vows to use his ESP ability to determine who altered his memories during his last mission.

But what he discovers might end up altering reality itself!

**For more information
visit:** www.SpeakingVolumes.us

Now Available!

"The best high-action thriller writer out there today, bar none."
—Jon Land, *USA Today* bestselling author

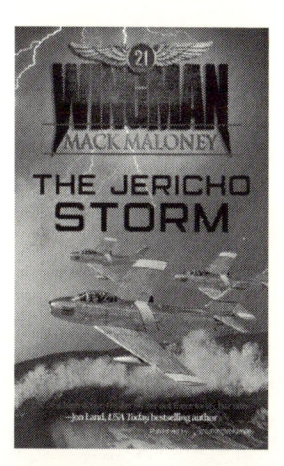

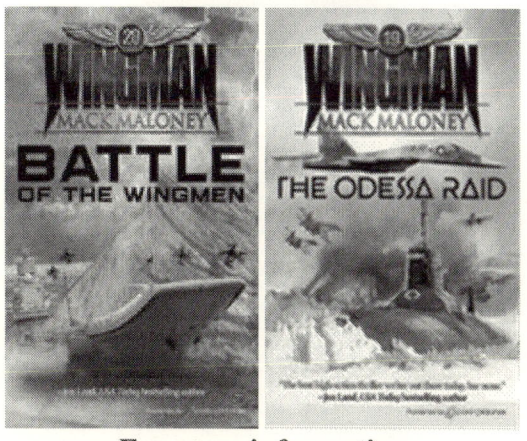

For more information
visit: www.SpeakingVolumes.us

Now Available!

CODENAME: STARMAN SERIES
BOOKS 1-3

**For more information
visit:** www.SpeakingVolumes.us

Now Available!

MORE EXCITING MILITARY/ACTION
BY
MACK MALONEY

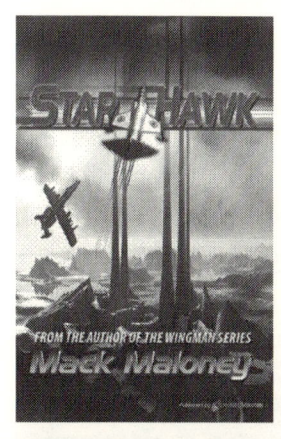

**For more information
visit:** www.SpeakingVolumes.us

Now Available!

IAN SLATER
WAR/MILITARY

**For more information
visit:** www.SpeakingVolumes.us

Made in the USA
Middletown, DE
09 April 2023